ANIMALS WE ARE

PREDATOR, PREY

VALERIE BRANDY

LITTLE LEO MEDIA, INC.

ISBN 978-1-7342792-2-1

This installment is Book Three in the "Animals We Are" Series.

Cover stock photo provided by Evgenii Leontev.

Photo of the author by David Mueller.

Copy Editing provided by Sharon Lennon-Mehlschau and Linda Triol.

Cover Photoshop provided by Aliimran24.

Printed in the United States of America.

Published by Little Leo Media, Inc.

To request permission to use passages from this book in any context other than a review, please contact the publisher at littleleomedia@gmail.com.

❀ Created with Vellum

*For all the readers who
Stayed with the adventure—
Thank you.*

*And, as always, for my Mom,
Who has believed in the adventure
From day one.*

ZOE'S POEM

LOGAN:

Meet me where the Bonds are kept,
　　　This Is where we'll start.
　　　A careful Sort of game we'll play,
　　　To open up your heart.
　　　We'll trace your present toward the past,
　　　No rock will go unturned,
　　　Don't think you know Much more than me—
　　　Your secrets I have learned.
　　　Don't wanna play? I dare you to,
　　　If You're man Enough.
　　　Giving up would look so bad,
　　　I thought you said you're tough?
　　　If you win a prize awaits,
　　　Lose, and I'll reveal
　　　Your secrets to the world at large—
　　　Your own fate you'll have sealed.
　　　So go to where this poem Leads,

If you're smart you'll know,
To tell them what the password is:
The place we met in snow.

— Z.

1

LOGAN

Paris, *France.*

I READ Zoe's poem beneath a streetlamp. Artificial light illuminates the hand-written characters, breathing life into familiar shapes. I've read the poem a hundred times already, but I look again, making sure I haven't missed anything.

The street lamps are scroll-like here in the second arrondissement— the French word for district. I'm a short distance away from the Louvre, where great works of art adorn the walls. But here I stand, investing my precious time in an amateur poem written by a silly girl playing with fire. It's ironic.

Zoe's poem— her invitation to play a game— was a cute attempt to mimic my own genius. Plebeian. Average. She doesn't have the subtlety I do.

That's the best you could do?

Still, I'm flattered. She's given me the opportunity to play my own game. Dared me to do it. It reveals a deep understanding of my psyche on her part. I would never turn down a dare. Not when she questioned my manhood. My courage. My ability. This is an opportunity to prove I really am better than those I've hunted. The predator's chance to live as prey, and emerge victorious once again.

No, I won't run. I'll play the game. And I'll stay two steps ahead, like always. Zoe believes she can change the dynamic between us, but even now I'm in control. I've hacked her phone. I know exactly where she is. I have access to her bank accounts. Her email. Her text messages. At any moment, I can pull the plug. Cut off her resources.

She is no threat to me.

Still, a single segment of her poem lingers, making the hair on my arms bristle.

> "We'll trace your present
> toward the past,
> No rock will go unturned,
> Don't think you know
> Much more than me—
> Your secrets I have learned."

My past doesn't exist. I deleted it long ago. Erased records on the internet. Made myself invisible. I was sad to do it. My exploits are varied, but exciting. It's a shame no one can know the depths of my brutality. The crimes I've committed. The power I've wielded. If we lived in a different world— one in which dominance was rewarded— perhaps things could be different, and my past could be celebrated. But we don't live in that world. So my past remains buried.

What does she know?

Nothing, most likely. I am ghost. A faceless fear. I've worked hard to present myself more as an idea than as a person. Just the way I like it. My identity lives within other identities, both metaphorically and literally. Ten different passports under aliases sit in my backpack, waiting to be used as a shield.

I move my backpack onto my other shoulder, resisting the temptation to sort through my identities. I like to imagine what trouble I could cause with them. What prey I could pursue.

But no. Today, I have one mission only.

My focus switches to the ornate building in front of me.

The bank *La Bismel* is one of many overwrought architectural monstrosities in Paris. It's a hunk of solid granite, featuring too many design details. Leaves painted on the balconies. Swirling curves carved onto the pillars. The French love their ornate architecture. Blame it on existentialism. If we all turn to ash in the end, might as well look at something pretty while we're here.

I know I'm in the right place because Zoe's poem contains a simple cipher. Certain words are capitalized to spell "Bismel." That, combined with her opening line "where the Bonds are kept," led me here after a simple location search for 'Bismel' + 'Bond.' Turns out, a scene from a James Bond movie was filmed in front of the bank. Zoe must of thought herself clever, noticing a double meaning between the infamous character and the financial product.

The bank has a sordid reputation. My research tells me the owner, Monsieur Bismel, is a man willing to lend without question if a potential customer meets simple financial qualifications. He doesn't care where the money comes from. Doesn't ask where it's going. It's surprising to me we haven't met before, given the nature of my work. Based on the information I downloaded about Bismel, he and I run in the same circles. We may not be associates, but surely we have some friends in common. No doubt, he would be my ally if I asked.

But no need for that yet. Today, I simply wish to access whatever Zoe has hidden for me.

I step into the street, crossing outside the lines. Cars redirect themselves. Horns honk. None of it bothers me. I learned a long time ago to claim my space in this world, everyone else be damned. When I reach the bank's ornate entrance, a steward opens one of the double doors for me. "*Bonsoir*—" he starts to say, but I keep walking, intent on one thing and one thing only:

Winning this game.

2

ZOE

*N*apa Valley, USA.

"YOU CAN'T GO ALONE," Mike says. We're fighting again. Lately, we do nothing *but* fight. The argument emerges in small doses— before bed, or at the breakfast table. It disguises itself as other things. *Who forgot to buy milk? Who left the front door unlocked?* A thousand tiny fights, all of them a piece of some bigger, impossible argument we can't resolve.

I shake my head, digging the toe of my boot into the gravel runway. We're standing at a private airport. A few hangars sit like domes. Most of the planes are small. Mine is the exception. "At least I'm finally gonna get to fly private."

Mike doesn't laugh. "I'm going with you."

"I need you to stay in California. To design the trap."

He sighs, bringing a hand to his temple. "Someone else can do it."

"It has to be you."

"It doesn't—"

"It does." I can't explain it to Mike, but he's meant to execute the final step in my plan to destroy Logan. He *destined* to do it. I've designed a trap to catch my prey, and he's going to build it for me. Plank by plank, board by board— we're breaking a curse. Mike building the trap that kills my nemesis will destroy whatever hex brought Logan into our lives. It has to be Mike.

"There's plenty of great carpenters out there," he reasons.

"Not ones who care as much as you." It's true. He's personally invested in making sure the trap holds. If it fails, I might not make it out alive. He's the only one I trust to do it.

Mike grimaces, practically pulling out his hair. "You have to let me come with you! We're a team, remember?"

Mike doesn't understand intuition the way I do. Doesn't have my sense of *where*. My sense of *when*. I've run a thousand scenarios through my internal compass. This is the only one in which we win.

"We have to split up," I say. "If we're together, he'll use it against us. Take one of us to manipulate the other."

"He can do that anyway!"

"No, he can't," I remind him, voice level. "He has no idea where we are. We're tricking him."

It's true. I knew Logan would track me from the moment he received my poem. To throw him off, I've hired two doppelgängers to camp out at our house in Los Feliz. It was expensive, but I'm putting Cassandra's money to good use. The doppelgängers have been going about our daily routines for us for the last three weeks. Using our credit cards to order food. Placing calls on our cell phones. Sending emails from our laptops. All while we stay safely here in Napa, in a guest house on a vineyard I rented with cash.

"I'm not choosing this," Mike says. His hands clench. Jaw tightens. "You made this choice alone."

"That's true."

"Married people don't do that."

"You're right," I admit. "I just don't see another way."

"So here we are."

"Here we are."

Behind us, a clanking noise interrupts the moment. The boarding ramp falls, revealing Oliver.

"But *he* gets to go," Mike points at my Mother's boyfriend, a retired pilot. Oliver is in his captain's hat, flushed and thrilled to be involved in an adventure.

"He's only dropping me off in Europe. After that, I'm alone."

Oliver smiles. "She wanted a real fighter by her side! Can't blame her, eh?"

Mike shoots me a look. "Is that true, then? You don't think I can keep you safe?"

"No," I say, fighting back a laugh. "Maybe I just don't care as much if Oliver dies."

"Hilarious," Oliver clucks his tongue.

"His eyesight isn't even good enough to fly!" Mike says, exasperated. "They made him retire over it and now you're just going to hop in a plane with him?"

"He's been flying my Mom all over the world, and she's fine," I shrug.

"That was a technicality!" Oliver interjects. "Just a little nearsightedness, that's all. We'll be fine. Most things we'd hit are far enough away I can see 'em. Most things..."

"What about the control panel buttons in the cockpit?

Those are pretty close up, wouldn't you agree?" Mike says, voice stern.

Oliver waves a hand in the air. "Got those programmed up here," he taps his head. "Don't need to see 'em. Little thing called muscle memory."

Mike rolls his eyes. "Thanks, Oliver, I feel much better now."

"Engines up in two minutes," Oliver says, heading back into the plane, grumbling all the way. "Kids these days."

Mike takes my hand in his. The look on his face tells me it's all become real for him. Up until now, he hoped he could talk me out of it. *Expected* he could change my mind. "Don't do this."

"I *have* to do this."

"Maybe I won't build the trap. This is your plan, not mine. If you won't let me come with you, I'll opt out."

He's playing hardball. It doesn't suit him.

"I can't make you do anything," I shrug, pretending I don't care.

"You're not prepared—"

"I've been training," I remind him. It's true. I've done months of combat exercises. Krav Maga, for hand-to-hand self defense. Kali, for weapons. A private tutor to help me get comfortable with a handgun. "I've survived him twice with no training," I say. "Now, I'm unstoppable."

"Can't you see it?" Mike says, dropping his arms by his sides.

"What?"

"You're acting just like him! Thinking you know it all. Arrogant enough to believe nothing can go wrong. Working alone because you don't trust anybody."

"I'm *nothing* like him." The words burn. Mike changes tact.

"I won't forgive you for this," Mike says, his eyes hard. "I will never fucking forgive you for this."

"That's fine with me," I tell him, letting the words sound as angry as I feel.

A rumble. The engines are up. I have to go. It stings to leave this coldness between us, but there's no other way.

Without really thinking about it, I turn and walk up the ramp, boarding the plane. I didn't expect it to happen so fast, but it's done, now. The ramp closes behind me. There's no going back. I take a seat, staring out the window at Mike down below.

His face is tight. Eyes wide. There's a jolt, and suddenly the plane is moving forward.

I lean back and rest my head on the seat, trying to forget that last look on Mike's face. What kind of person says goodbye the way I just did? The image is burned on the back of my eyelids. Mike's eyes, so filled with hurt. What if I never see him again?

Maybe what Mike said is true. *Maybe I am acting like Logan.*

I don't mean to, but I'm crying now. Hot, heavy tears roll down my cheeks, betraying everything I can't let myself feel.

Suddenly, the forward motion stops. Oliver pops his head out of the cockpit.

"Bloody moron blocked take off," he points out the window. There's Mike, waving his arms in front of the plane.

"Let down the ramp."

Oliver does. Mike's already at the bottom, hands in front of him as if to say *I-didn't-do-it.*

"I'm not trying to stop you," he says, face flushed. "I just couldn't leave it that way. Not like that. Not with you. Not if this might be the last time we—"

He doesn't get to finish his sentence, because I'm already

down the ramp. In one smooth motion, I put my arms around his neck and picks me up, wrapping my legs around his waist. He kisses me, and I realize very suddenly the weight of what it means to be responsible for each other. Until death due us part.

Mike rests his forehead on mine. "I love you," he whispers.

"I love you," I tell him.

Then, I walk back up the ramp, trying not to look over my shoulder at the only person who could make me stay.

3

LOGAN

P*aris, France.*

MY WATCH LIGHTS UP as a new hour strikes. I've been here thirty minutes. That's fifteen minutes too long.

At a bank like *La Bismel*, it's not a good sign to be kept waiting. Important clients are always ushered forward with the utmost sense of urgency. I'm used to being treated like a V.I.P. at most financial institutions, not just as a result of my large holdings, but because of my powerful work connections. I work with men who aren't as sophisticated as I am. Men who will kill first and ask questions later. The banks know this about me and treat me accordingly. But now— thanks to Zoe— I'm sitting cross-legged on a plush couch in the lobby, waiting. Waiting like a plebian. Like an ordinary, everyday Joe.

Don't they know who I am?

Of course, they don't. No introductions or names were necessary. I simply told the bank attendant the passcode I ascertained from Zoe's poem. It was easy to figure out. Zoe's letter was hardly a cipher.

> *"If you're smart you'll know,*
>   *To tell them what the password is,*
>   *The place we met in snow."*

The password was *Yosemite.* The place where I almost had her. The place where she showed her worthiness as an opponent. I'd always suspected she'd be an exhilarating conquest. It was there— in the snow-covered hills, far away from the city lights— that Zoe proved herself to me.

Yosemite. The word sends and electric current rushing through my veins. I remember the location with the same fondness others feel when they recall a trip with a lover. When I whispered the name of the place to the bank attendant, it tasted like chocolate liqueur on my tongue, promising new adventures to come.

I've been waiting ever since.

"*Monsieur,*" the attendant reappears from another room — one of many in this maze of a building. He motions to a metal door. It's one I assumed belonged to a vault. "They will see you now."

My only response is a nod. This measly attendant doesn't deserve anything more. I follow him to the metal door. He unlocks it with a key and allows me to proceed alone. The moment I'm inside, the unmistakable jangle of keys echoes from outside. The attendant has locked me in.

It occurs to me that Zoe might not have any elaborate plan at all. Perhaps she's lured me to a secure location to allow others to do her dirty work for her. To assassinate me. To deprive the Earth of my presence in one gory, butchering swipe.

No. She wouldn't underestimate me that way. Zoe knows I'm prepared for every situation. My eyes close as I picture the gun in my backpack.

When my eyes open, I take in my surroundings with practiced patience. The room is solid metal on all four sides, but the bank has tried to soften its prison-like aesthetics with the luxury their clients are undoubtedly accustomed to. Two chairs are outfitted with plush textiles, organized around a solid wood table painted in gold leaf. A bottle of champagne and two glasses sits on the table. A thick carpet covers the floor, soft beneath my feet.

Perfect for muffling sounds, I think, staring at the hideous shag beneath my shoes.

My eyes dart to the far wall, which is decorated by a mirror. The frame is carved from swirling, solid wood, painted in the same gold leaf as the table. The frame is meant to distract— to make the glass look removable. But I know better. That mirror is built into the wall. Double-sided glass, clearly. Someone might be watching from the other side. Someone I can't see.

The zipper on my backpacks whines as I pull it open, removing my phone from within. I've rigged it to operate almost anywhere in the world. The phone is its own hotspot, capable of hijacking any satellite to create a signal, even in places so remote there's not a tower around for miles. But despite this, the upper right hand corner is blank. No bars.

This room must be secured against all intrusions, physical and technological. It's a cone of silence, the kind usually reserved for top secret conversations in government facilities wary of espionage.

What bad company is Zoe keeping? I smile to myself.

Another jangle of keys echoes from outside the door. It

opens, and a polished woman enters, carrying a briefcase. She's wearing a blue pant suit with metallic buttons. The suit looks heavy. The weight of the fabric tells me it's well made. Designer.

"*Monsieur,*" the woman holds out her hand.

"In English," I say, not because I don't speak French. But because want to make it clear this meeting will be held on my terms.

The woman grimaces. "Absolutely. Anything for the guests of our customers."

The way she emphasizes the word *guests* makes an angry acid bubble up in my throat. It's as if she's reminding me I'm here at someone else's bequest. Images flood my brain with ideas. Ideas about what I would do to her, if I had the time. How I'd hunt her. What I'd take from her. Where I'd bury the body.

She sits at the table. Motions for me to do the same.

"I understand you're here to play a game," she smiles.

"Perhaps," I answer. "I'm still waiting to see if the rules are to my liking." Little does she know, the entire world is my game.

She nods, hitting a button underneath the table. As if by magic, a secret compartment opens. There's an electric whir as a small television monitor emerges, parking itself on top of the table.

"Understand," the woman continues as if she does this sort of thing every day. "The bank *La Bismel* is not responsible for the contents of any blind transactions. We guarantee privacy on behalf of our clients, and I cannot provide you with the name, address, or information of any of our customers."

"I don't need her address," I snarl.

"*Trés bien,*" the woman responds, cheerful. "Your presence in this room and continued participation in this trans-action indicates that you agree to the terms of our facilitation, most notably that you do not hold La Bismel or its associates liable for any damages you may incur."

She slides a paper across the table. Tiny font outlines the bank's terms and conditions.

"We'll also need a signature," she states, placing a pen in front of me. "Use any name you like."

She knows I'm a ghost, I think. Of course, she'll still need a signature. Not because it means anything. Just to prove to the bank's legal department that she tried.

"Fine," I say, signing the page with a simple letter L.

She takes the paper back with a smile.

"What is it the Americans say?" She chews on the inside of her cheek. "Ah, yes. 'It will do.'"

With that, she pulls another form out of her briefcase, placing reading glasses on her crooked nose. "A certain client of ours, who wishes to be referenced only by her first name—"

"Zoe," I say.

"Yes, Zoe," the woman confirms. "This certain client of ours would like to invite you to play a game. She has called it, 'Predator, Prey.'" The woman pauses, looks up for my reaction. I don't give her one. "You followed a clue here, correct?"

"Correct."

"Excellent," she answers. "Then you understand the premise."

"I *built* the premise," I spit. The woman ignores me.

"You will follow clues to various locations deemed 'important' by our client. If you complete the challenge at each location, you will be rewarded with another clue. If you complete the *final* challenge, you'll win back what you've lost."

"I haven't lost anything," I say.

"Oh, *suis-je bête!*" She shakes her head as if she's just remembered she's left the oven on. "My mistake. I should have opened with this."

She hits another button under the table and the television monitor clicks on. The image on the screen makes my heart pound. My stomach and throat switch places, hot, heavy blood draining from my face.

There, on the screen, is a flickering black and white image of the only thing in this world that's valuable to me:

A large, beaten up suitcase. One I've had since I was a child. I know it's mine because two letters are engraved on the front. Letters from my real name. The one I was born with.

Zoe knows who I used to be. The thought rocks me.

My eyes turn back to the screen, riveted. I'm unable to look away. The suitcase is sitting on a platform in what appears to be a vault. The walls are solid metal. The floors smooth. There's an air-vent up above, but it's too small for any human to fit through. The image has the uneven, low definition flickering of a CCTV security camera.

"Is this in real time?" I ask, hardly able to believe what I'm seeing. That suitcase was under lock in key a location no one can access but me. How Zoe got to it is a mystery. How she *knew* about it is another.

"Yes," the woman confirms. "It's being held in one of our underground, secured facilities."

My brain goes into hyperdrive, plotting ways to circumvent the game and retrieve the suitcase myself. Maybe I can break into one of their vaults. I've completed harder tasks.

As if the woman knows what I'm thinking, she adds, "All

of our vaults are impenetrable. They're air-tight. No human could even breath within their confines. Retrieval of items is completed by machines only. To authorize mechanical removal takes an eye scan, a fingerprint approval... and then there's the issue of *where*—"

"You don't know *where* it is?" I scowl.

"We have 87 different mini vaults scattered around the world," she smiles. "The locations are hand-written on paper, to avoid hacking attempts. We had encrypted them previously, but—"

"Encryption is useless," I slump back in my chair, waving a hand absent-mindedly. "Should've used something off-network."

"You work with computers?" She asks, curious.

"I thought you didn't ask personal questions."

She shakes her head. "I can ask them. I only cannot provide answers."

"Lovely," I snarl, pulling my chair closer to that monitor. The image is real. It has to be. Still, I'll need to check to be sure.

"What's inside?" The woman asks, once again treading into personal territory.

I run my hand over the screen, thinking about the suitcase and the objects within. I've done a myriad of illegal things in my life, but I've been careful not to leave a record. I've scrubbed the internet of my presence. Left no trails leading back to me. Except one. This suitcase.

Inside are what I like to think of as "souvenirs." Objects taken from people who wronged me, on whom I took my revenge. With each conquest, I stole something to help me remember the experience. Something that allows me to relive the memory when I hold it in my hand.

They say all criminals want to be caught, but I've never

believed that. I didn't save these small souvenirs because I wanted to be caught. I saved them for posterity, but also as *proof.* Proof of my brilliance. My most creative, most powerful deeds have had to be carried out in secret. In silence. In shadows.

No, criminals like me don't want to be caught. What I've wanted is *acknowledgment.* For someone else to recognize my brilliance. To see my genius. I'm a rare species of predator. One that hunts not needlessly, but with a sense of justice. When I choose my prey, it's because they've wronged me in some way. I am an equalizer, and my deeds serve to tilt the scales of power in my favor.

The small trinkets inside that suitcase are evidence of my superiority. They're proof that I can control the world around me, and bend it to my will. Realign it in my favor. They're more than just tangible reminders of my most exhilarating experiences. They're objects that make me feel safe, because they prove to me that *I am in control.* Those who wrong me will *always* get theirs in return, because *I make it so.*

In addition to the souvenirs I've collected, that suitcase holds the ghosts of my past. My original government-issued i.d. My passport. My family lineage. I never burned them, because I wanted to remember where I'd come from. Wanted to remind myself what I learned as a child. That I can only count on *me.*

Now, those faint traces of who I used to be are piled next to objects connected to multiple crimes. That suitcase could ruin me, and it's now under my enemy's control.

"*Monsieur*?" The woman is staring at me, eyes wide. She's concerned. I'm not sure why until I realize I've moved across the room. I'm standing still, staring at a wall, totally unsure how long I've been there. I'm not blinded by rage. No, I'm numbed by it. Empty.

My plans for Zoe were grand in the beginning. I thought she had the potential to be like me. To come around to my way of seeing the world. To join me in pure, existential self-fulfillment.

But now I see. She's must be destroyed. When I end her, I'll take a button off her blouse, adding it to my collection, to my suitcase of souvenirs.

I unclench my fists and walk back toward the bank representative.

"You have something else for me, I presume?"

The woman nods. Removes an envelope from her briefcase. Another clue. I take it.

Urgently, the woman waves a hand at the mirror on the wall. There's a jangling sound outside, and the door unlocks. I stride out of the vault, but stop before I reach the exterior.

My body turns to face the woman, moving on its own without any instructions from me. "You asked what's inside the suitcase?"

Her face says she regrets it.

I smile at her. "Maybe, one day... you'll find out." With that, I stride out of the bank, determined to make Zoe pay.

4

ZOE

Geneva, the Franco-Swiss border.

It's night when our plane lands on a dirt airstrip outside Geneva. This small airport is a blip on the map, privately owned and perched on France's northern border with Switzerland. It's little-used, but most who do come through are rich diplomats visiting the CERN research institute who prefer to fly private. And then... there's me.

Outside the plane's window, red signal lights flash in an uneven rhythm, marking the edges of the runway. The signals remind me of a lighthouse— the pitch black night around them an endless sea.

"Your mother wanted me to try one more time to get the number for your burner phone," Oliver says as he lets he down the ramp.

"Can't," I tell him again. We've had this conversation every hour since we left. "Too big a risk. It'll make her a target if she caves and calls me. Outgoing calls only. I'll reach out when I can. You'll stay at the safe house with her?"

Oliver nods. "Cassandra nabbed us a house on the island," he says, referencing the very unexpected financier of my expedition. "She's quite determined to put the worst of herself towards something good. Keeps talking about how she and Francois have right proper plans for the museum. Bloody hell. The way she describes it, it's the next MET."

"Sounds like her," I say. My bag suddenly feels heavy on my shoulder, and I'm eager to get to my next location so I can get on Geneva time. "Thanks," I tell Oliver, holding out my arms. He pulls me into a hug.

"Can't talk you out of it either, I suppose?"

"Nope," I confirm.

"In that case, don't tell your mother I said this, but—" Oliver looks around as if my Mom might have secretly stowed away on the plane. "If anyone can beat him, you can."

He's said the thing I needed to hear most. I'm not big on hugs, but I give him one more anyway before proceeding down the ramp. "Take care of her," I call over my shoulder. He gives me an earnest solute.

There's only one hangar in this airport, so there's no place for surprises to hide. Still, the hair on the back of my neck bristles as Oliver taxis the plane toward the hangar for a refuel. If Logan *does* know what I'm up to, he could have men waiting in the hangar to intercept the plane. I say a silent prayer that Oliver makes it to the island safely.

Up ahead, a small, flat parking lot marks the end of the airport. It's paved in asphalt. Lit by two flickering poles that offer a soft, blue glow. There's only a few cars in the parking lot. One of them will be mine.

Just then, the door to a black town-car opens. A driver in a hat steps out.

"Zoe?" He asks, his accent something I can't place. I nod, heart pounding. I won't relax until he says the words that let me know I can trust him.

He unfolds a paper. Reads a line written there. "Who would've guessed that a wolf and a bee might become friends?"

I smile. This is the secret passcode Cassandra and I agreed upon. "Only the Great Everything," I say, offering the planned response so the valet knows he has the right person. He grabs my bag and puts it in the trunk before opening the door for me.

"Miss Cassandra sends her regards," He revs the engine and carries me away from the airport, plunging our little car into the dark, twisting road ahead.

We drive for hours. No pit stops. No bathroom breaks. The landscape changes, but our little car remains the same. A silent bullet streaking past the best of France, carrying two strangers who don't mind staying that way. The valet doesn't ask me any questions. I'm happy not to have to think of answers.

Mile after mile, shallow grass breezes past my window. Tiny flowers dot the open fields. The flowers might be lavender, but I can't tell, because everything looks the same in the dark. Off in the distance, the lights of a city gleam. I imagine that it's Paris, but I'm not sure. I don't know North from South, or East from West, here.

What a terrible way to see France, I smile to myself.

Five hours go by, and I know we're close when the temperature of the air changes. I've been assured the tinted windows of this vehicle are reinforced with bulletproof glass — a safety precaution Cassandra and I agreed upon before my departure. Still, I risk rolling one down a little. The scent of the ocean floods the car, familiar and crisp. The salt makes my lungs open wide. We're finally at the coast. It won't be long, now.

I know it's time when the valet turns his headlights off. We're invisible, now, no longer a bullet but a ghost, careening down a dark road at the edge of a little village. We pull up to a barn in the back of an unnumbered house. The valet exits the car, pulling open the barn doors. Then, he drives the car inside. The engine clicks off as he gets out to shut the barn doors in our wake. Now, we're locked inside, alone.

"No one followed us, yes?" He asks me the question without making eye contact.

"No one," I say. My eyes were glued to the rear window during the last ten minutes of our drive, so I know it's true.

The valet walks to the other side of the barn, where another car lies in wait. He rips off a dusty cloth cover, revealing an old Renault 5 Turbo. The outside looks its age, but I know the inside has been rigged with the fastest engine money can buy. It's fully-loaded within, but not much to look at without. Kind of like me.

The trunk makes a popping noise when the valet clicks it open. He lifts up the mat. Underneath is a deep compartment, housing a handgun, a sniper rifle, and a plastic bag. Inside the bag is a collection of paperwork— documents, in my new name.

I open up the bag and pull out an American Passport with the name "Melanie Schneider" written inside. There's a picture of me from a few years ago within. I wonder if Melanie is a real person who doesn't know her identity has been used to make a passport. The idea makes my stomach turn, but I don't have time to dwell on it.

"All is good, yes?" The valet asks.

"Yes," I tell him. He nods. Passes me the key to the Renault.

"There's a map," he says, pointing to the bag. "It will tell you how to get to Marseilles."

"Thank you," I say. He shrugs like I'm a customer at a cafe and he's the barista. This is just a job to him, and he only cares what I think because he wants satisfied customers. I'm surprised by how much I like that. No niceties. No need to explain myself. To him, this isn't personal. For me, that's freeing.

"Tell Miss Cassandra how happy you were," he says as he hops back in the town-car. He speeds away from the barn. His brake-lights disappear down the road, and I'm suddenly very aware of how alone I am.

I slip into the driver's side of the sports car, touching the steering wheel with reverence. It's a powerful thing. It occurs to me I should've started it while the valet was still here. What if it doesn't work?

Relief floods over me when I put the key in the ignition and hear a soft purr from the engine. I *will* tell Cassandra I'm happy. It's amazing what money can buy.

Keeping my headlights off, I pull away from the barn, heading toward the sea. Marseilles promises not just answers, but a friendship. Someone who knows what it means to be hunted by Logan. Someone who can tell me everything I want to know about him.

The coastal drive flies by, and in less than half an hour, I've reached Provence, the county that houses Marseilles. When I pull up to the small, sea-side town, it smells like fish and lavender. An odd combination.

It's quiet this late. The engine rumbles as I pull into a parking spot in front of an ancient apartment building.

That's one of my favorite things about Europe. Five-hundred-year-old buildings house people with computers and cell phones.

Without hesitation, I stop at the steps and press a button on the callbox for entry. "Hello?" a voice on the other end says. She sounds, even though she's expecting me.

"Who is the predator and who is the prey?" I ask her, once again using a passphrase. There's a long pause on the other end. I wonder if she'd deciding whether or not to let me in. Maybe she's thinking of backing out.

Then, the voice in the callbox says, "Whoever is hungrier."

There's a loud buzz from the front doors. I grab at the handles before she can change her mind, pounding up the steps to a unit on the third floor. My eyes dart across the hallway, making sure no one else is in the hall. When I'm sure the coast is clear, I knock three times.

The door opens, slowly, painfully. Behind the security latch, one big, brown eye looks back at me, reminding me of the heavily-lashed eye of a cow.

"Gabrielle?" I murmur. Neither one of us can believe the other is real. We've never met face to face. Only over messages and phone calls. Certain, now, that I am who I say I am, she opens up the door and lets me into her apartment.

If what Gabrielle has told me in her emails is true, I'm the first one to enter in over a decade.

GABRIELLE LAYS A STEAMING pot of tea on the table between us, with cups to match. The handle on mine displays a small pattern of flowers, each one different from the other. They must be hand-painted.

"*Grand-mere's*," Gabrielle says, pointing to the set. "My Grandmother's. It was one of the few things that survived the fire."

As she bends down, her blouse slips off her shoulder, revealing uneven skin. Burn marks, all across her back. I've only ever seen her on Zoom. The marks are more obvious in person. She catches me looking.

"It's fine," she says. "I find them beautiful now. *'Jolie Laide.'* So abrasive in form they become pretty. They're a part of me. Something visible that shows I've survived. Other people have invisible burn marks within their spirits. Mine are... apparent."

She pours us both a cup of tea. "Thank you," I tell her.

"I must admit, I was quite afraid this was a trap." She looks away from me when she says it.

"You still are," I say, making it a statement— not a question. "I'd hoped the articles would help..."

When I reached out to Gabrielle, I sent her evidence to support my claims about being stalked by Logan. I provided newspaper articles from Yosemite. Clippings of local reports from the Seychelles. A picture of Mike and I being loaded into an ambulance. Still, it's not enough. And I understand why.

She shrugs. "Once something terrible happens to you, it's hard not to look around every corner. That's why I don't let people inside my apartment. Or at least, I haven't. Until now."

"You can trust me," I say, even though I know it doesn't mean much. I reach into my bag and pull out a collection of line drawings, laying them out on the table for her to view. "The puzzle you constructed is brilliant." I point to the last part of the sketch. "I've had our team follow it to the letter. No changes."

She shrugs. "Once an engineer, always an engineer."

"It has to relate strongly enough that he makes the connection. Maybe if you told me everything, gave me the details..."

"I've told you enough," she says.

"You've told me the cliff-notes," I object. "I'm not trying to pressure you. I just don't want to get this wrong. It's important. Important that he knows it's from you."

She stares into my eyes, like she's searching for something. "You are looking for someone to place the blame?"

I shake my head. "No," I tell her. "He already knows I'm behind the game. He'll blame this entirely on me. But it's imperative he understands he can't outrun his past. I need him to know this puzzle is personally designed by *you*."

Gabrielle sighs. "If you fail, and he kills you, he'll come after me next. If *you* found me, he can."

"Maybe," I tell her, unable to be dishonest with someone who is so much like me. "But I don't intend to fail."

A moment. She finishes her tea. "We worked together at C.E.R.N.," she begins. I already know this, but am afraid to interrupt her in case she clams up. "We were colleagues. He became infatuated with me, and when I rejected his advances, he burned down my home. The puzzle is at C.E.R.N. He'll know it's tied to me."

"He'll know it's *tied* to you," I counter. "But how will he know you *built* it? If it's not personal, he'll think I just dug into his past. It's supposed to be personal. That's an essential piece of my plan, of what we're doing here."

She looks at the curtains. They're blocking the window. No way to see outside. I can't help but wonder how often she keeps those curtains closed. How often she blocks out the rest of the world.

"C.E.R.N was looking for the best electrical engineers in

the world to upgrade their system," she says, still looking at those curtains. "Not just in the country. Not just in Europe. The best in the *world*. I was one of those."

"And so was he?"

She nods. "We were both just twenty-two. Fresh out of college. I had a masters already. Skipped ahead by finishing multiple years at the same time. He didn't have a masters, but he didn't need one. He'd spent his life in front of a computer. Technology was his passion. He'd attended Columbia. Went to college in the states, even though he was born and raised in Germany."

"What name was he using when you met him?"

"Johann Grentz," she answers. The back of my arms prickle at hearing the name aloud.

"You might not know this, but you're one of the last people to have met him while he was still using his birth name," I tell her.

She smiles, rueful. *"Ja'i de la chance!* I have all the luck."

Clothes and receipts brush my fingertips as I search through my bag, trying to find what I'm looking for. Finally, my fingers find again the binder. I pull it out and flip through the pages. It's my master file on Logan, a.k.a. "Johann."

"Here," I tell her, flipping the page around. "Johann disappears after the fire at your apartment. He never used the name again. C.E.R.N. was his last real job. Since then, he's been working for international criminal organizations. Helping them set up dark web networks to evade Interpol. He's the premiere technician for covering up your footsteps, creating unbreakable back-channels to communicate without being observed—"

"You sound... *impressed*," she chastises. The comment throws me.

"I'm not," I tell her. "I'm just trying to understand what makes him tick. You can't combat an enemy if you don't know what motivates him in the first place."

This seems to satisfy her. She pours another cup of tea.

"When we worked together, he started off friendly enough. We formed a sort of kinship. Always laughing over the same humor. But he became more and more insistent. Entitled to my time. I noticed he seemed to think the world was against him. He perceived the slightest rejection as a personal affront. He seemed unable to acknowledge others are having any right to make their own decisions. To him, people were more like..."

"Objects?"

"Yes. A means to an end. On the days where he asked too much of me— too much help with his work, too much time declaring his brilliance— I'd tell him he was treating me like the vending machine. Put a quarter in. Get what you want. Although I didn't even get a quarter."

"But you still thought he was just a normal guy?"

She shrugs. "A normal man with some issues, yes. It didn't get strange until the roses arrived."

"The roses?"

"*Oui.* I was married, at the time," she adds. "I mentioned to Johann that my husband always bought me wildflowers, even though I'd ask for roses. It was a joke between my husband and me. 'You can never make me happy,' that sort of thing. I told Johann about it in passing, and not a week later, roses appeared at my doorstep. Not one, but hundreds. Day after day. An endless stream. My husband thought I was cheating on him. It created problems in our marriage. I suspected Johann but when I asked him about it, he denied knowing a thing."

"Did his behavior change?" I ask.

"No. He just carried on like normal. But I'd notice he showed up unexpectedly. At the *marché des fremiers*. The market I frequented, even though his flat was across town. On the bus. I was certain I was losing my mind. Started doubting myself. The worst part was, we still had to work together."

"That must have been—"

"*Absolument*," she answers. "He was my supervisor, as well. He would ask me to dinner. I would say no. He'd do the same the next day. As I rejected him, his anger grew. Then, the day arrived. We were to give a presentation in front of all of C.E.R.N. The president of the systems division was present. I'd been working on a new coded security panel that was supposed to open and close a door based on finger-print recognition. Cutting edge at the time, not so much anymore. Back then... It was the biggest opportunity of my young career."

"Not with him there," I say.

She grimaces. "When it came time to present the new security framework I'd designed, the electrical panel was completely out of order. The wires had been mislabeled. Everything was in the wrong spot."

"He sabotaged you?"

"*Oui*," she nods. "I attempted to fix the damage but it was impossible. In my original framework, each wire had a color assigned to it. A color that hinted at its connectivity. He changed the labels. It would have taken days to figure out. I am certain it was him, because after the presentation, he asked me... '*Quel fil? Rouge ou blu?*'"

My French is terrible, but I get the idea. "Which wire, red or blue?" I translate. She nods.

"He likes puzzles," I say.

"I certainly hope he likes this one," she smooths down

the page in front of her. It outlines the details of the puzzle we've set up for Logan. "He will know it's me," she says, pointing at the final segment. "There."

I look at the page and immediately understand. "Yes," I agree. "He'll know it's you."

There's a long pause in which neither one of us speaks. My mind whirs, trying to find a way to bring up a topic I've been avoiding.

"You believe your husband died in the fire Johann set?" I ask.

"The dental records of the body they found matched," she says, surprised.

"Yes, but that doesn't mean he died *in* the fire. I think Logan— I mean, Johann— killed your husband and then lit the fire to cover up his tracks."

Gabrielle puts a hand to her mouth, horrified. "When I arrived at our home, it was already burning. I ran inside, but the worst was already done." She pauses, thinking. "This changes the puzzle. I need to make adjustments, for him—"

"It's done," I say, waving a hand. "I re-wrote the poem. I figured you wouldn't mind."

"Good," she says, distant.

"I don't know if you feel better knowing, but you deserve to hear the truth. Remember when I told you I stole something from Johann? Something he values..."

"Yes," she says.

"It was a suitcase. He kept mementos from his victims. It's how I found you." I reach into my bag, pulling a gold wedding band from a pocket within. "The engraving led me to you. It was your husband's?"

She takes the ring, turning it over in her fingers like she's looking at an archeological marvel from a thousand years ago.

"The engraving was an address," I say. "A house. When I looked up the owner, your husband's name came up. From there, I found the news of the fire, and..."

"Me," she nods. "And how you found my phone number?"

I figured this would bother her. Gabrielle's internet records show she's made every effort to disappear. She's in a self-imposed witness protection program. The apartment we're sitting in is leased under someone else's name. Most likely a sympathetic relative. There's no job information listed. No social media. I'm not surprised she's troubled by the ease with which I located her.

"It was expensive," I say. "Don't worry. It wasn't easy."

She doesn't say anything. Just turns that ring around in her hands.

"Why was the inscription your home address?" I ask her, trying not to let my voice reveal that I don't find it particularly romantic.

"We lived together before we got married. His family wasn't French. They looked down upon our cohabitating at the time. Wanted him to marry someone closer to home. But it was living together that made us realize how madly in love we really were. That house meant a lot to us."

She puts the ring on her finger. Stands. Surprises me by walking over and sitting down next to me. The closeness is startling after how aloof she's been.

"*Merci*," she says, putting a hand on my shoulder. "I am happy to have the ring back."

"Of course," I tell her. "There's one final matter. The job..."

"I want it," she says.

"It's for dangerous people. Doing very bad things," I remind her. "It's not making the world better."

"Neither is a fortune 500 company," she says. We've had this argument before. The job was her idea, not mine. And I'm still not sure I like it.

"I'm not sure they'll agree," I tell her.

"Then they don't agree," she shrugs. "But you promised me this, so you must try."

A sigh escapes my lips. This is the part of our deal I like least. I want nothing to do with this arrangement, but I did promise. We both know it's a promise I won't break.

"I'll try," I nod, gathering my things. As I head for the door, she stops me again.

"Zoe?"

"Yes," I say.

"Let me know when it's done." She's looking at those curtained windows again, like she's wondering when she'll finally be able to let in the light.

"I will," I promise. It's another one I won't break.

5

LOGAN

P*aris.*

ZOE's next clue stays in my backpack on the journey home. I don't remove it on the train. Don't bother to crack open the envelope it as I step onto the platform. I just leave it there, deep in an interior pocket. I imagine it as a snake. A living, twisting pet I carry with me.

It's strange, being back in Europe on Zoe's command. I've returned as an adult, but always for business. Always with a purpose in mind. I've never allowed myself the time to look around, to marinate in the places I used to know. I have so many memories here. Memories of my childhood. Memories I'd like to burn, along with Zoe's letter.

Did she choose to send me here to weaken me? To throw me off my game by bringing me back to the place where I buried the old me?

A buzzing sound emanates from the box in front of me. I'm standing outside a safe house in Paris. I've entered the gate code wrong. I'm distracted. Exactly what Zoe wants.

My lungs expand as I take a deep breath. I enter the 16 digit code again. The code is the same for similar safe houses all around the world. I've memorized it in chunks. The only way most human beings can retain information longer than a phone number.

Click. The box in front of me buzzes, and a light on top turns green. It opens, revealing an old metal key. I extract it, using it to unlock the deadbolt. Then the knob. Then an extra latch.

When I enter the safe-house, it looks exactly like the others I've stayed in. Decorated in neutral tones. Beige drapes. Heavy textiles. Everything is shades of taupe and grey. There's a flatscreen TV on the wall. A quick investigation of the refrigerator reveals a six pack of beer, a block of cheese, creamer for coffee. The freezer is better-stocked. There's a collection of microwave meals, some frozen burritos, a take-away pizza. Criminals aren't known for their cooking abilities. The men I work for don't concern themselves with the beauty of life. They only care about ending beauty. Squashing it beneath their boots.

I roll my eyes in disgust. I may work for brutes, but I myself have more refined tastes. I appreciate beauty. Enjoy owning it. Relish turning transforming it beneath my tutelage, teaching it to become a beauty that serves me and only me. It's a quality that makes me an excellent chef. I can take stale bread and a few basic ingredients and cook a five star meal, exactly to my tastes. It would've been nice to find a few essentials in the fridge, but no matter. We work with what we have.

I grab a beer from the refrigerator. It crackles against my throat with a familiar tingle. The label tells me it's *Beck's*, a

German brand. At least they had the good sense to pick a decent brew.

There's a remote control sitting on the end table, and its presence reminds me: I need to make sure I'm not interrupted. A button on top doesn't match the others. It's a different shape. Different size. There's a picture of a lizard branded on the button's surface— the insignia of the organization I work for. I grab the remote and raise the curtains on the window, looking down at the street below. The call box sits at the steps, waiting. I point the remote in its direction, and hit the button with the lizard insignia. With a dinging sound, the light on the callbox turns red.

Sorry, comrades, I think. *This one's taken.*

The red light serves as a subtle messages to other traveling employees of the organization I work for. It let's them know this safe house is unavailable. Even though we're on the same team, we don't enjoy running into one another when we can help it. We're terrible company, even to each other.

Good. Now I can rest. I can read Zoe's clue, and truly begin my journey. Feet up on the table, at ease because I know I'll win, I tear open the envelope with my teeth, and begin to read.

∾

You'll go back in time,
  like particles can,
  This is the place,
  That made you the man.
  Where France and Switzerland,
  Meet on the edge,
  To work here? A vow

To science you pledged.
But this time you won't be
On the main floor
Try the spare knob
On the maintenance door
Take a trip down
To level fourteen
Look for the flowers
You know what I mean
Follow the petals,
To find your next clue:
Hope you can tell
Red wires from blue.

THE BEER I'm drinking turns to acid as I read the last line of the poem. "Hope you can tell red wires from blue."

She knows.

Somehow, Zoe's dug so far into my past she knows about Gabrielle. About the fire. She must have spoken to Gabrielle personally. Gone to Marseille and found her sad little apartment there. Gabrielle thinks she's disappeared, but I know exactly where to find her. I watch the place occasionally from a satellite I've hacked into. See Gabrielle's lithe figure cross the window on the rare days she opens the curtains. Sometimes, she looks into the distance through the window frame, like she senses I'm watching her. She probably wonders why I've let her live if I know where she is.

It's because you're already broken, I'd tell her if she asked me. *There's nothing left to destroy.*

And yet, a surprise. Zoe has tracked Gabrielle. Enlisted Gabrielle's help. Raised her from the dead. *Exhumed* her, in a resurrection of sorts. There's no way she would have referenced the wires otherwise. Zoe has reignited Gabrielle's flame. I'll have to extinguish it again when all this is finished. No matter. A task for another day.

And C.E.R.N. She's sending me to C.E.R.N. The place that chose me to work for them because of my incredible aptitude. The place where I realized I was destined for bigger things. That, if I wanted my talents to be recognized, I'd need to go to those who wouldn't punish me for my differences. Wouldn't scold me for my nature.

I shudder at the thought of returning to C.E.R.N. Not because I'm afraid, but because it represents the mediocre life I would've had if I'd continued working there. Endless meetings in human resources, being asked to explain my "behavior toward my colleagues." The team at C.E.R.N. hired me because of my incredible aptitude, and then expected me to make my methodology more palatable to others. I wasn't allowed to shepherd my co-workers into greatness. The head of human resources told me I was wrong to tamper with the work of others, using words like "sabotage" and "obstruction." What she didn't understand is that I was only helping them get better. If the work is only average, only sufficient, then what better way to grow except through trial by fire? Nature says it's true. Rocks become beaches when challenged by the elements. When I tampered with the work of my peers at C.E.R.N., I was only leading them to greatness. Trying to push them from high school science-fair level engineering to something groundbreaking. Something magnificent.

No one at C.E.R.N. understood greatness. Understood the cost of becoming great, like me. Still, somewhere deep inside, they knew my reasoning was correct. Even as they reprimanded me for supposed interference, for alleged harassment, they let my co-workers go over time, firing them one after the other. But they never fired me. No, I was too valuable. Too talented. It was *me* that left them. Still... it's not a place of happy memories.

My stomach turns at the thought of going back. Zoe thinks she can dig into my past and not pay?

Think again.

There's a landline sitting on the end-table, rigged through a cord in the wall. To ensure the location of the safe house is secure, it's untraceable. It hums as I pick it up and put it to my ear, dialing yet another number I've memorized like my life depends on it.

After a few rings, the number leads to an artificial intelligence recording. It's one I've programmed myself. This is my own mailbox, a phone tree of sorts I can use to get in touch with the most important connections, all from one number. I like to imagine it as a customer service line, except it's been created by me, for me.

"Press 1 for Sylian," a female, pre-recorded voice says on the other end.

No, I think to myself. *Sylian cannot know what I'm up to on his dime.* He thinks I'm busy buffering our physical firewalls, double-checking servers across Europe. He likes me to check my own work twice a year. Every time he asks, I lie and tell him that I'm on it, charging him for the service even though I haven't done a check in at least 36 months. What Sylian doesn't understand is that my work is immaculate. It doesn't need checking.

"Press 2 for ammunition. Press 3 for location resources. Press 4 for man power."

I press 4. This is a line that connects me to a specialized crew of men at my disposal whenever I need physical backup. They're the brawn, not the brains. They know not to ask questions, and merely react to my instructions. They're trained marksman, and quite capable in an unarmed physical altercation. They do my bidding, like dull, stupid extensions of my own two hands. Right now, I have them stationed on Mike and Zoe, following them 24-7.

Pick up, Smith, I think, listening to ring after ring. Finally, Smith answers.

"Hello," his voice is warm and slow on the other end. It sounds like his mouth is full. He's probably eating. Unbelievable.

"Pull the plug," I tell him. There's a long silence on the other end. I think I hear chewing.

"You're sure?" He swallows.

"No," I practically shout. "I'm joking."

Another long pause. "So I shouldn't do it, or—"

"Let me be literal, as sarcasm is clearly lost on you," I scowl. "After you finish your fucking sandwich, take your guns and the other guys, march in that fucking house, and push them in the car. Take them to the nearest safe house and hold them until I get back. Don't let anyone see you. Obviously. And don't tell Sylian."

"Why can't I—"

"Because Sylian doesn't want to be bothered with the minutiae. That's what he hired me for. And he put me in charge of you, so that you wouldn't bother *him*. Got it?"

"Got it," Smith says. There's another long silence. He won't hang up until I do. Always awaiting further instructions.

"You're still eating, aren't you?"

"You said to finish my sand—"

Click. I hang up on him mid-sentence. There's nothing I despise more than stupidity. And as much as I hate that she's dug into my past, I can't help but admire Zoe for her wit. It's what drew me to her in the first place. She's smart. Not as smart as me. But smart. She could be great, if she'd let the right person mold her.

I roll over on the couch, clicking off the lamp on the end table. I'll sleep here instead of the bed. I like to stay alert in these safe houses. Despite the name, they never feel all that safe. Not really. The darkness envelopes me as I lay still, thinking of Zoe and the lengths she's gone to for me. I imagine what we could've been, what we could've done, together, if she'd only let me in.

P *rovence Airport, France.*

SUITCASES CLICK OVER TILES. Flight numbers flood across the intercom system. I tune it all out, focusing on the impending journey.

My flight to Croatia will be a short one. From the south of France, I'll only be in the air an hour-and-a-half. By any measurement, this should be an easy travel expedition. Still, my heart pounds as I scan my passport. My new identity, "Melanie Schneider," could be flagged by Interpol. What if someone else has used it in the past for nefarious purposes? I'll be hauled away for questioning, shoved into a cell in some undisclosed location, unable to carry out the rest of my plan. Mike will have to hire international human rights lawyers to bail me out, undoubtedly biting his tongue to keep from saying, "I told you so."

The airport attendant looks up at me. Compares my face to the photo one on my fake passport. There's a still, breathless moment where I'm not sure what's going to happen, but then— he lets me through.

My lungs relax as I exhale. If Interpol doesn't have a flag out on my fake identity, it's unlikely Logan is tracking it either. Maybe I'm truly anonymous. Maybe my plan is working.

Despite my earlier success, my heart still pounds as I board the plane and click on my seatbelt. As the plane rises into the air, I think about the lengths Logan will go to in order to get revenge. Would he take down an entire commercial flight just to get to me? My eyes scan the plane for any suspicious people, any suspicious packages. Nothing stands out as unusual.

To distract myself, I pull out my burner phone. There's wi-fi on this flight, and it seems as good a place as any to make a one way call. I've been instructed not to let any call last longer than two minutes, less it become traceable.

Mike picks up on the first ring. "You okay?"

"Everything's fine," I tell him, speaking quickly so as not to waste our time. "I met with Gabrielle. I'm heading to the next location."

I can practically feel Mike's finger running down the itinerary I left him. It's a list of each location on my trip and when I'm expected to be there, along with contact names, phone numbers, and addresses of where I'll be. He laminated it before I embarked. It's a hand-written copy. No digital versions exist, because Logan can hack computers. Better to go old school and keep it offline.

"Roger," he says, not saying the name of where I'm headed out loud. "Remember to take in the walls." I smile. Mike's already told me about his college trip to Dubrovnik and the magnificent walled cities there.

"I will," I say. "How are you?"

"Miserable," he answers honestly. "But working on what you wanted."

"How's it coming out?"

"Good," he says.

"Better than good," I tell him. He's the best carpenter in the world. "You can make something out of nothing."

"I hate to admit this, but this *might* be the most complicated, perfect thing I've ever made," he says.

"See?" I laugh. "If my life depended on every piece of furniture you carved, your business would really flourish."

"That's not funny," he says, and I picture his scowl. It's rare to see Mike scowling. A frown always looks wrong on his face.

"How's my Mom?" I say, changing the topic. A flight attendant comes by with a drink tray. I shake my head, ushering her on.

On the other end of the line, Mike sighs. "She's fine but she can't understand the two minute call limit. She keeps talking and talking right up until I have to hang up. So far I've heard about the weather, and the food there, and she even asked me if we want her to mail back some souvenirs like we didn't almost die there—"

"She's nervous," I tell him.

"I know," he says. "So am I. Zoe, I—" He pauses, like he's thinking about the right way to say something. "Do you remember when you were leaving and I said you were being like him?"

My chest tightens. How could I forget it?

"Yes," I say.

"There's... I wanted to tell you that I didn't mean it the way I said it. What I meant was... Don't take this the wrong way but you *do* have some things in common."

"This isn't making me feel better," I say.

"What I mean is you're both smart. You're both strategic. You're both aloof, and don't trust others very easily. But there's something that you have he doesn't. Something that sets you apart."

"What?" I ask.

There's a beeping sound from Mike's end. He's set a timer to let him know when we're close to the limit.

"Time to hang up," he says. "When you call your Mom, make sure you track the time, because she won't," he laughs.

"What sets me apart from him?!" I ask, wanting to hear it from Mike.

"Too late," he says. "I'll tell you next time we talk. It'll be your encouragement to call me," he teases.

"Ten seconds," he adds, urgent.

"I love you," I say.

"Love you," he says. I click off the phone. Taking it away from my ear is physically painful, but I have to be smart. I have to trust in our love enough not to need the reassurance of a longer call.

I settle in my chair, but I can't get comfortable. A sudden loneliness washes over as I think about what Mike said.

Did Logan pick me because I'm like him?

To push the thought away, I grab my phone and make another call. My Mom. She also answers on the first ring.

"Honey!" She exclaims, launching into her speech. As she talks, I set a timer on my watch to two minutes. "Oliver and I have been all over the island. Francois and Cassandra have been lovely tour guides. They've showed us the entire town. What a beautiful place! This is a much better experience than last time—"

"Last time we were in the Seychelles we were almost murdered," I remind her. The woman on the seat next to me does a double take. I smile at her like I was joking. She puts on her headphones. Scoots away.

"That's true," she acknowledges. "That really did ruin the trip." There's a pause. "Are you safe?"

"I'm safe," I tell her. "Cassandra did a good job. Money really buys you the best protection in the world."

"Thank God," my Mom lets out a sigh of relief, then launches back in to talking a million miles a minute. "Just don't do anything stupid. We've been enjoying the beach here but I'm being careful. Haven't swum too far out. Please do the same. When you come back, when it's all, um— *over* — maybe we could all rent a cabin somewhere. Get a bit of down time. Wouldn't that be nice? I've been learning to make a new kind of Cheesecake, I just know you'd love it—"

"Mom?" I ask. She stops.

"Yes, honey?"

"Do you think I'm like him?"

"Like who?"

"Logan."

There's a long pause. She's thinking about it.

"Not in any way that matters."

Just then, my watch beeps. We've reached two minutes.

"I have to go, love you," I say as quickly as I can. I hang up the phone before I can hear her say "I love you" back. It crushes me to do it, but I tell myself that I know she said it, because she always says it.

It's not long before there's a popping in my ears, and the unmistakable feeling of the plane descending. The wheels hit the runway, and I pull my bag from the overhead container. We've finally reached Croatia.

When I go through customs, my passport works again without issue. I grab my bag, and go to the airport parking lot, searching for the vehicle I've been assured will be waiting. As I check license plates, I imagine what it would feel like to be here on vacation instead of a mission. I'd love a plush hotel mattress, and the ability not to look over my shoulder.

The license plate in front of me belongs to a black BMW. I double-check the number against a paper in my hand. The numbers match. This is the one. The trunk pops open when I wave my key-fob in front of it, and I throw my bag inside. In no time at all, I'm zooming across the Croatian coastline.

A winding road curves around a sheer cliff face, kissing the edge of the sea. The turns are tight, a hairpin's flip. I hazard an occasional glance below, where the waves are so small they look like flowing lines of lace on a blue gown. One wrong turn, and I'll drop straight into the ocean.

In another time I would have taken my foot off the accelerator, but today, I can't risk slowing down. There's an important contact waiting for me— one who won't like it if I'm late. This man is the most important piece of the puzzle I've designed. He will help me disassemble Logan. Not destroy. Just take apart. I don't enjoy the thought of causing harm, not even to my enemies. My goal is to reverse-engineer Logan. To take him apart, piece by piece, and let him look at himself.

The road dips down and suddenly I'm circling the walled city of Dubrovnik. Cruise ships dot the harbor, anchors laying heavy beneath the water. Tourists click their cameras. Sun-hats abound. It's a warm, beautiful day.

The walled city looms before me, reminding me of a massive castle. Many years ago, the Croatians used these walls to protect themselves from coastal travelers and traders who might attack the city. There's a drawbridge at the entrance, and I wonder when it was last raised.

The car purrs as I pull into a parking spot. I march over

the drawbridge, looking for the place I've been told we'll meet. I can't help but stare upward as I enter the walled city, noting the ramparts. Mike was right. The city is incredible. When we first started dating, he told me getting to know me felt like entering Dubrovnik for the first time. I had my walls up.

The bridge pours me out into the city center. Restaurants offer al fresco dining. Cobblestone streets peel off in every direction, saddled between three-level buildings. Surrounding it all are the walls. Suddenly, I feel claustrophobic. If a tidal wave rose from the ocean and flooded the city, there'd be no way out except over that bridge. The crowded, bottle-necked bridge. In an emergency, evacuation would be impossible.

Eager to get this over with, I spin in place, looking for the meeting spot. My eyes note a clock tower in the distance— the city center. I walk toward it, trying not to draw any attention to myself. There's a pair of college students taking pictures in front of the tower. When they're finished and I'm sure they've gone, I walk toward it, searching around the back. Finally, I find it, right where they said it would be. A small maintenance door in the back.

I open it and slip inside, startled by how cool and soft the air is within. There's a stale, dusty scent. The kind of smell that tells you this door isn't opened often. My eyes scan the areas. The room I'm in is a circle, mimicking the exterior shape of the clock tower. A winding staircase leads upward, but also down. So far down I can't see to the bottom. Before I can wonder what lies below, there's a creaking sound from behind me. The door opens again, letting in blinding sunlight for a moment before slamming shut.

Two men stand in front of me. They're six feet tall. Much heavier than me. Arms the size of tree trunks.

"Hello, boys," I smile, trying to seem like I do this everyday.

"How sharp are the teeth of a wolf?" One of the men asks. Another passphrase I've developed.

"By the time you find out, it's too late." I provide the necessary answer.

The first man nods at the second. He approaches me, a cloth bag in hand. I knew this part was coming. But I'm still dreading it. He puts the bag over my head, and I let him, because it's the only way to get to where I need to go.

The men lead me by my elbows. I can't see anything behind the light-blocking cloth. "Watch your step, one says." We descend. I can only assume we're going down those stairs, into the dark abyss below.

Step after step, we continue for what feels like miles. Suddenly, the ground evens out. It feels hard beneath my sneakers, like solid concrete. There's the faint scent of gasoline, and I hear the familiar beep of a car door unlocking.

We're in a parking garage. It must be located beneath the clock tower, known only to those in a certain inner circle. Certainly none of the tourists above us are aware of its existence.

The men usher me into the backseat, forcing my head down and clicking my seatbelt on for me. Then, the car takes off. I feel a sinking in my stomach as we rise higher, and I wonder how long it will be until we're back above ground. Suddenly, I'm grateful for the bag over my head. Better not to know.

We drive for what feels like an eternity. I try guessing at the time passing, but can't keep my numbers straight. I count from zero to sixty, gauging the minutes. Ten minutes pass. Twenty. Now I've really lost count. My breath is sticky inside the bag. I'm inhaling my own carbon dioxide.

How much longer?

Finally, the car stops. The sound of the door opening behind me makes my heart pound. We're here. I've done it. This is the most dangerous step in my plan. The biggest risk. I'm counting on Logan being dispensable. I'm betting on the fact he doesn't have a real friend in this world. That there's no loyalty among thieves. If there is, I'm already dead.

The men pull me out of the backseat, leading me somewhere. I can feel the sun on my face for a moment, but then it's gone again. A door shuts behind me. I'm inside now.

They pull off the bag. My eyes scan the room. It's solid concrete. Grey walls. No windows. Practically a prison. I don't know if it's a lone structure, or part of a bigger compound. I have no idea where I am. It's plain, and oppressive. The kind of place you'd bring someone you plan to torture.

But in the center of the room sits a solid wood table, decorated by an ornate tablecloth. A man sits there, eating fruit from a tray. He's not very tall. Maybe five foot five. But the expensive clothes he's wearing show that he's in charge. A mustache sits above his upper lip, and his hair is thinning in the center. On his right ring finger is the biggest ring I've ever seen in my life. It's a single band with a metal circle perched on top that's the size of a quarter. Engraved on its surface is the image of a lizard, tail curling, a forked tongue poking out of its mouth.

The man smiles at me like we've known each other for years. "I must admit, I did not expect you to make the trip," he says, making me wonder if he means he didn't think I'd have the courage, or if he's implying he didn't expect me to *survive.*

"I never break a promise," I say.

"That is good. *Prego*," he answers. His accent is Italian, and I wonder if it's real, or if he is like Logan. A chameleon. Someone who will change into whatever animal benefits him most in a given moment. "I never forget those who keep me waiting."

He motions to a chair at the end of the table. I sit. There's a plate and a table setting in front of me. The man watches, waiting. I take a piece of fruit and put it on my plate as if I plan to eat. This seems to appease him.

"I like my guests to be comfortable," he tells me.

"Is that what I am? A guest?" I ask.

"You don't feel as much?"

"The bag didn't help me feel comfortable."

He shrugs. "Guest. Informant. See it as you will. You have nothing to fear here. I always appreciate those who offer me useful information. Still, precautions must be taken."

"I understand," I say.

"Now, onto business," he continues. "I've investigated the claims you've made about one of my employees. I must admit, at first I did not believe you. But it appears you're onto something."

"Yes," I smile at him. "Yes I am... *Sylian*."

LOGAN

G*eneva, just outside C.E.R.N.*

THE FRANCO-SWISS BORDER doesn't have much going for it. Rolling hills. Some sheep here and there. I've always thought that people make too much of natural beauty, and this boring, quaint part of Geneva is exhibit A. Who wants nature when you can sit inside a concrete building with internet access and working bathrooms, safe from the elements?

I'm sitting in my car with the headlights off. The night feels especially dark after leaving behind the bright lights of Paris. My eyes still haven't adjusted to the nothingness around me.

There's only one sign of human civilization out here, and it's impossible to miss. A spherical ball of warmth, blinking at me just a few hundred yards away.

C.E.R.N. The letters stand for the "Conseil Européen pour la Recherche Nucléaire," an organization formed way back in the 1950s with the intention of investigating the ramifications of Nuclear power. Today, everyone's forgotten about the council's origins. All they know is that the large hadron collider might discover new worlds, entire universes exiting on a micro level we can't see.

Of course, I never cared about any of that. I took the job at C.E.R.N. out of a desire to use my talents to make the most money, with the least effort, and maybe gain a little nuclear knowledge at the same time. A knowledge that eventually led me to my current and far superior employment.

My eyes scan the horizon, noting the familiar spherical shape in front of me. The facility doesn't look like much from the outside. Just a strange, artistic bubble, lit golden in the night, blooming from the Earth like it wasn't built by man. The Hadron colliders sits within. But what's most important is underground. Beneath the golden fishbowl turned up-side, multiple stories burrow deep into the Earth. Control rooms. Servers. Maintenance tunnels. Dark rooms where decisions are made. All of it lies beneath the Earth. A maze of hallways allow for the facility's functioning, the people within like a thousand tiny ants keeping the whole thing running. I used to be one of those people. Now, I'm the snake that destroys the anthill as he burrows into the ground.

The car door shuts behind me, and I try to muffle the sound of it shutting. I walk into the night, heading toward the golden orb. The light it emits grazes my skin, making me eager to escape to the caverns below, where the darkness used to make me feel right at home.

The spherical facility at C.E.R.N. is protected by multiple security measures, both physical and computational. I know, because I built half of their online systems myself. Those don't stand a chance against me. But the physical security measures— those are another matter.

There's a long, cement driveway that leads up to the sphere's entrance. From the outside, the place looks open. Vulnerable. But within, multiple armed guards protect the building from threats. Terrorist organizations. Nuclear power deniers. Crackpot conspiracy theorists who think the hadron collider is going to accidentally open a portal to another world filled with dangerous beings. Name the threat, and I guarantee you it's been sent to C.E.R.N.

My backpack pinches my shoulder-blade as I hike it higher on my shoulder. The walk down the cement driveway is long. There's too much time to think. To reconsider.

I've prepared myself to pass the interior security check— the most dangerous part of my expedition. After that, it'll be smooth sailing. I fish a badge from my pocket. I printed it last night, using the document scanner in the safe house. It was easy enough to hack into the C.E.R.N. main-frame and browse through the current employee list. When I built their system, I left myself plenty of backdoors. Secret ways to re-enter that only I can use.

The badge displays a picture of a man that's about my height, with my coloring. His name— according to the employee directory— is "Ronald Summers." In the photo, the man has a full beard, which helps make his overall appearance less specific. I've mimicked it, growing my own beard to match. In the picture he's wearing a base-ball cap, and so am I. Our similar builds and facial structures aren't the only reason I chose him. He's also useful to me because he works the day shift, and I knew I'd be here at night. With any luck, we won't run into each other. A bigger risk, perhaps, is passing someone who knew me when I worked here. I'll have to keep my head down.

A glass door slides sideways and offers me entrance. I'm inside a familiar, circular room. Tile floors. Impossibly high ceilings. It's build like a cathedral. A church of scientists.

Two guards are standing by the metal detector. They're talking to each other in French. I don't bother trying to translate every word, but think I hear something about a woman, and a date gone wrong. Without making eye contact, I toss my bag on the X-ray table and step through the metal detector. It doesn't buzz. I'm through. On the other side, a guard passes me my backpack. He barely looks the scanner. They've gotten lazy, and it's to my benefit.

Up ahead, a woman smiles at me, holding a scanner to check my badge. Suddenly, I regret choosing to visit the facility at night. Normally there'd be a long line of people waiting to scan their badges, but tonight, the place is vacant. Empty. It's too easy to notice what's different. Too easy for some busybody to discover I'm not Ronald Summers.

The woman lifts the badge of my shirt and holds the scanner to the barcode. She's about to pull the trigger, when she pauses, considering. She looks at the picture. Looks up at me. Looks at the picture again.

"Manchester United?" She asks. For a second I'm not sure what she means, but then I do a double-take at the picture. Ronald's baseball cap. It's got the logo for the Manchester United Football Club.

The woman nods at the cap I'm wearing in real life. "Or City?"

My heart sinks as I realize what's happened. The cap *I'm* wearing features the logo for the Manchester *City* club, but in the photo, Ronald's wearing a cap for Manchester *United*. The two groups may share similar names, but they're bitter rivals. Any real fan would know the difference. But last night— when I was printing the logo at the safe house in the late hours of the evening, exhausted and angry— I didn't note the difference. I lost focus. Cut corners. Didn't live up to my usual standards. I've made a grave error.

The woman locks eyes with me.

"Don't tell my wife because she's a Manchester United fan, but I'm hedging my bets," I say.

There's a moment, then the woman bursts out laughing. She winks at me, scans my badge, and sends me on through.

I don't exhale until I'm at the elevators. It's difficult to admit I've executed this with less perfection than desired. This is not my usual standard of excellence. Still, if it's anyone's fault, it's Zoe's, not mine. She's made a game too elementary for my skill level. There's no challenge, here, and any mistakes I make are only the result of playing at a lower level. Yes, this game is not sophisticated enough for me. The predictability is making me lazy.

I check Zoe's poem for the next instructions.

> "Take a trip down
>   To level fourteen
>   Look for the flowers
>   You know what I mean."

This would be easy, except that there *is* no fourteenth level at C.E.R.N. The floors are all underground, and they end at thirteen. The only thing below level thirteen is a set of access tunnels, hardly used except for housing a network of pressure-sensitive cables.

The elevator button lights up as I hit the button for the thirteenth floor. There's a whooshing feeling in my stomach as it drops down into the Earth. Deeper and deeper, like I'm tunneling toward the Earth's core.

My descent stops. The doors open, and I spill out into a tiled hallway. The air down here feels crisp and cold. A byproduct of being pushed through a constant filtration system. This space is so far underground, all metrics must be controlled by man. The temperature. The air flow. All of it's calibrated to perfection by human minds. Some people might feel uneasy down here, but not me. When I worked at C.E.R.N. my coworkers commented on struggles with claustrophobia. They feared what would happen if the ventilation system stopped pumping air into the lower levels, or what might occur if a sudden Earthquake struck. But none of it ever phased me. I appreciated the artificial environment. The creation of something immaculate where only chaos existed before.

As I make my way down the hallway, I glance at the row of doors in front of me. Behind each one, I know there's rows of servers, collecting valuable information from the experiments conducted just a few floors up at the Hadron Collider. The Hadron collider is 100 meters underground— floor number ten— and only a few floors are located beneath it, including this one. Floors 11, 12, and 13 are the less frequented areas in the structure, and all three of them are dedicated to electronics. Keeping equipment underground is an excellent way to avoid heat interference. Luckily, I won't have to worry too much about running into anyone down here. Only technicians visit the server rooms.

I proceed to the end of the hallway and make a hard right, where I finally find what I'm looking for. A metal door, nondescript except for the hazard sign on the front. There's a lot of hazard signs around here, and after awhile, your brain starts to ignore them. This one is bright yellow, with a warning on the front: "PRESSURIZED. DOOR LOCKS BEHIND YOU." The line beneath reads "MAINTENANCE ONLY." There's a post-it underneath that with a hand written message. "**Keys?**"

Good God, I think. *The maintenance team must have locked themselves down there at some point. Idiots.*

There's a data sheet posted next to the door. It lists specific instructions for entry and exit. A quick read tells me an alarm will sound if the door is left propped open for longer than five minutes, because the tunnel's pressurization requires equalization. Only a code entered on a keypad can override the auto-lock and alarm mechanisms.

Closer examination of the handle and the seal around the door reveals it's airtight. Although I've never been down there myself, I know the maintenance tunnels are home to immense stretches of electric wires and cables, all of which power the facility and transmit information. The tunnels are like freeways for data, which connects from below to the serves in the surrounding rooms. They're kept pressure regulated to ensure proper functioning of sensitive equipment. The smallest change in temperature or pressure could affect the data being sent back above.

I reach into my backpack and pull out Zoe's poem again, remembering a line that stood out to me.

> "*But this time you won't be*
> *On the main floor*
> *Try the spare knob*
> *On the maintenance door.*"

My eyes scan the door again. There is no additional knob. Just the sole handle that will lock automatically behind me once I'm in. But then, I notice something that shouldn't be there. The wall is constructed from plain, ceramic tile, but one tile is different than the others. On its corner is a hand-painted image.

An image of a rose.

Gabrielle.

My fingers trace the tile, and it moves a little in response. It's loose. With some digging, I'm able to break apart the surrounding grout, which looks like it's been purposely left half-complete. The tile pops out in my hand, revealing an empty hole behind it. Inside the hole sits an electric screwdriver, and a new handle. One that I assume is not programmed to auto-lock behind me. The meaning of Zoe's poem clicks into place.

> *"Try the spare knob*
> *on the maintenance door."*

It's clear what I have to do.

Impressive, I think. Zoe must have bought off someone who works here. Someone willing to go above and beyond for some extra cash.

My watch beeps as I set a timer for five minutes. Then, my hand closes around the electric screwdriver, and I get to work. In no time at all, I'm pulling off the old doorknob and replacing it with the new one.

I consider trying to test it, but there's no way to do so without propping the door open and triggering the alarm. I'll just have to take this one on faith. A glance at my watch tells me I have less than thirty seconds left. I step through the open door, and let it shut behind me. For a moment, there's nothing but a still, quiet darkness. Not frightening, but peaceful. My fingers close around the handle. If it doesn't turn, I'm trapped. But it *will* turn. I know it will, because I know Zoe. She's in it for the sport. For the message. Not for an easy kill.

The door opens with a swooshing sound, just like I knew it would. Before shutting it behind me, I grab a flashlight from my backpack and use it to illuminate the space. At first, I don't see anything unexpected. Only huge bundles of wires running the length of the tunnel. But then, I shine the light toward my feet and discover a trail I'm meant to follow.

She made it from rose petals. Red, curling petals line the tunnel, pointing me in the way I'm meant to go. I laugh out loud to myself. Quaint. Adorable.

The rose petals take me down a set of stairs, and then deeper into the tunnels, moment by moment, turn by turn, always reliable. A right. Then a left. More cables. Finally, the space opens up into a safe harbor of sorts. It's an electrical panel in a carved out section, set back from the main tunnel to form its own little room. A single, dangling light hangs from the ceiling. On the back wall is an electrical panel, with various cables shoved into respective pegs. It reminds me of one of those old telephone operator panels they'd use to connect callers to one another.

At the top of the panel, there's a box that looks like it doesn't belong. It reminds me of a tiny safe. It looks like it could open. Wires are blossom from within. On top sits a rolled up piece of paper, encircling a single, long-stemmed red rose.

My hands reaches for the flower, and I pull it from the piece of paper, unrolling the letter. It's handwritten. Like they wanted this to be personal.

> "*Now your fate,*
>   *Is up to you,*
>   *Solve this puzzle,*

To gain a clue,
If your love
Was really true,
It should be simple,
To remember who—
You harmed with hands,
In fire, too,
You took his life,
Now he'll end you.
Spell the name,
Of the one you took from me,
If you can remember?
Sincerely,
— G."

My blood runs cold. There's a terrible pounding in my chest. When I set fire to Gabrielle's home, I'd hoped it would look like an accident. I didn't expect *her* to believe as much, of course. I knew she'd have her suspicions. But I hoped I'd create enough doubt to always leave her wondering. Now, Zoe's discovered not only that I set the fire, but that I killed Gabrielle's husband with my own two hands before a single match was lit. Before the lighter fluid was even poured, he was already dead. How she knows this, I can't be sure. But it makes me wonder what else she knows.

I re-read the poem and examine the wires in front of me. Most of the holes in the panel are filled, but there's five at the top that are empty. Each wire has been assigned a tag with a letter on it. A quick survey makes it clear: the wires serve as letters of the alphabet. One tag is marked "B." One is "C." One is "Z."

The game is straightforward enough. I'm to pick five

wires to place in the empty holes, spelling the name of Gabrielle's husband. This would be simple.

If I remembered his name.

When I killed him, I didn't care. He was nobody to me. Nameless. Not a person, really. Just an empty object. A way to get what I wanted. A way to harm Gabrielle. I never considered him as anything more. Just collateral damage. It's strange, now, that retrieving my suitcase might rely on knowing something about him.

My legs walk on their own accord, moving me in circles around the room. My memory for codes and numbers is excellent. For details about people, not so much. Still, the information is in there somewhere. I try to remember what Gabrielle said about her husband. She was French, so he must be French as well. It's likely, isn't it?

There was something about being French, I remember. Something she mentioned about their families.

I grab the wires and spell out a common French name, inserting them in the holes.

P-I-E-R-R-E.

Buzz. The box emits a sound that goes downward in tone, letting me know I got it wrong. Suddenly, I notice there's a screen on the front of the box. A timer appears. Three minutes. I've activated it now, and there's no undoing it.

Think, I tell myself, watching the numbers descend. I'd assumed this puzzle would rely on intelligence, but instead it's dependent on something else. Some investment in paying attention to the lives of others that I don't possess.

Past interactions with Gabrielle flash before my eyes. The way she invited my criticism of her work. How she appreciated my input; until, of course, she didn't. The roses. The flowers. She'd mentioned her husband didn't give them

to her often. There was a reason. She blamed it on something. Something about him.

*That's what she said about him being French... That he
wasn't.* The memory is jarring. *He wasn't romantic, not in the
way she was used to. Not like the Frenchmen she'd dated in her
past.*

The conversation comes back to me. She was standing
by the coffee bar. Babbling on. I was thinking about something I needed from her, when she made the complaint.
And then she told me... she said...

It hits me. *His family didn't like them living together before
marriage.* Because they were from America. Evangelical, she
said. Very religious. They wanted them to marry before
cohabitating.

Her husband was American. Possible names play like
flashcards in my mind's eyes. Evangelical might mean
Southern. Or perhaps a name with biblical origins?

Gabrielle's face swims in my imagination, and the image
becomes clear. I'm swept back to years ago, to that conversation at the coffee bar, surprised at myself for paying enough
attention to be able to recall what she said. "Jacob doesn't
buy me flowers," she smiled at me. "It's the only way in
which he is a bad husband."

I cringe a little at the way she emphasized the word
"only." Something about it felt like an accusation, at the
time.

A glance at the timer tells me I have fifteen seconds
left.

Jacob. That was his name. It has to be right. It's very
American, and biblical. My memory is good. I decide to
trust it.

I put all the letters in place, but pause when I go to pick
the wire labeled "A." There's not one wire, but two. The first

is red. The second is blue. Both are labeled with a tag marked by the letter "A."

Which wire, red or blue?

It's a gut punch. They must think they're cute, Zoe and Gabrielle. The two of them, gathered together. Talking about me. *Laughing* at me. But when I'm through with this, they will pay. They'll regret being so flippant. They'll regret using my past against me.

Three seconds left. I grab the red wire and shove it in the second hole for letter "A." A silent pause. Then, the buzzer sounds. I've picked the wrong one. The timer runs to zero.

Above me, an alarm sounds. The pressurization alert. The timer on the box must be connected to the spare handle. The second it activated, the handle must have sprung open, leaving the door "ajar" by the security system's standards.

I'm out of time. I grab the other wire for "A"— the blue one— and shove it in the hole. The metal box opens. I take the envelope within, swing my backpack over my shoulder and run from the tunnels, following the trail of rose petals back toward the door.

Shouts fill the hallway. Someone will be waiting for me when I reach the exit. But they won't be ready for the predator they're about to encounter. Thoughts of Zoe and Gabrielle— sitting together, brainstorming ways to attack me— consume me. I will tear them limb from limb for this, and destroy what makes them feel alive. The spark with in each of them will be extinguished by my hand, whether physically or otherwise. But, for now, I take my rage and channel it ahead of me, toward the door to level thirteen and whoever is on the other side.

8

ZOE

Dubrovnik, *Croatia.*

TEA TIME IS OVER. It was brief. An abrupt, strange greeting ritual. Now, Sylian walks me through his compound, giving me a tour like we're old friends. He trusts me. I don't like his trust. I haven't earned it. Somewhere deep down, I feel as if it will come with a cost.

"Over here," Sylian points down the hallway at a set of stairs. "The steps lead to where we make our own wine."

"You don't buy it?" I ask.

"Too many sulfites," he shakes his head. "We have a vineyard in the back."

We round another corner. This place is all hallways and doors. No windows. No light. But otherwise, it seems like a relatively normal place of business. It's an international operation, with people of all origins walking the halls. I've heard at least three different languages in the past five minutes. So many people from different places, all united by a common cause. The idea would be romantic, if the cause weren't organized crime.

The day to day rhythm of the place mimics an ordinary company. I've seen a cleaning person go by, pushing a cart. Two women walking the halls, chatting. Some men leaning up against a wall, talking to each other as if they're catching up on weekend plans. They looked completely average, until I noticed the sniper rifles swung over the shoulders.

"Here, the ammunition." Sylian points at another room. Inside, the walls are lined with weaponry of every kind. Grenades in a mesh organizer. Guns organized by shape and size. It's overflowing.

"Interesting," I nod, as if he's just shown me where bathroom is.

Another left. Sylian unlocks a door, revealing a dark-room that houses a network of computers. Servers line the back wall. Wires everywhere. Overhead, a single light flickers. Behind a set of monitors sits a man in his mid thirties. He's wearing a plaid shirt over his lanky frame. He looks out of place compared to the broad, muscular guards that roam the hallways.

"Tell her, Alanzo," Sylian says. The man jumps. Reaches for my hand. Shakes it.

"Nice to meet you," he says. "I did some digging..."

"*Today,* Alanzo."

"Right, well, your information proved to be quite accurate, actually."

"Logan left backdoors?" I ask, heart-pounding. This is the moment of truth. I made an educated guess about Logan's job performance using information from Cassandra's hired informants, and my own understanding of his psyche. Today, I find out if I'm correct.

"Plenty of them," Alonzo says, pulling up an image on

his screen. "There's gaps all over our firewalls. Places where someone who knows what they're doing could get in. They're intentional. Constructed. You'd have to know where to look. But he's left them there like ghosts within the software."

"He wants access in case you ever let him go," I say to Sylian. "I'd venture to guess C.E.R.N. also has a security problem they're unaware of.

Sylian waves a hand. "I expected as much. This is not what angers me."

"You're not *mad* about that?"

Sylian shrugs. "Standard practice. What's to keep me from killing him except a little insurance built into his work? No, no, that does not bother me." He looks at Alonzo. "Tell her."

Alonzo's fingers fly across the keyboard. He pulls up what looks like an expense report. There's a list of equipment. Private plane tickets. Meal and travel expenses. Ammunition. Technological expenses. Wires. Cables. Telemetry systems.

"He's been embezzling money. These expenses over the past few years— the travel, the equipment— all of it was supposed to be done with the purpose of performing maintenance on our global systems. Checking on our server rooms in different countries. Providing tech support at our international safe houses. But then I cross-referenced the logs and it looks like he has even performed a simple systems check in over three years."

"How often was he supposed to be checking it?"

"At least every six months," Sylian answers. "Per my instructions."

"He's spent enough money to buy his own island," Alonzo rolls his eyes. "And if he wasn't spending it on keeping our I.T. flowing, what the hell was he using it for?"

"Stalking me," I say. My voice comes out dry and sarcastic.

"Yes," Sylian flushes, his face angry. "Playing games instead of taking care of business. I can understand insuring his work, but time theft... that's another thing."

It's difficult not to respond when Sylian reduces Logan's stalking to time-theft, but now is not the time. I keep my thoughts to myself. Sylian turns to me.

"You've done an excellent job. For quite some time, I've wanted to hire an auditor. To monitor all our operations."

The idea throws me for a loop. "That's not why I'm here," I tell him.

"Alonzo," Sylian says. Alonzo understands what he's asking. He leaves the room, pushing his chair out and closing the door behind him.

"You do not want a job. You don't want a favor. What is you want?" Sylian asks. "No information comes free. At least, no *useful* information comes free."

"I want my life back," I tell him. "Logan's hunted me. Tried to hurt the people I love. I want to walk through the world without fear."

"Consider it done," Sylian says, removing a cell phone from his pocket. "I'll have my men take care of him."

"No," the word comes out louder than I intended. "I mean, I've got it."

"You've... 'got it?'" Sylian asks, bewildered.

"It has to be me," I say. "I need to know that it's finished forever, and the only way to be sure is if I'm the one who does it."

"Fine. We'll bring him here. You can watch."

"That won't be necessary. Logan is currently... occupied,

and I like that way. He'll show up where I need him to be, *when* I need him there. I have it handled."

Sylian looks me up and down like he's trying to solve a puzzle. "Then what is it you need from me?"

"At the right time, in the right way, I'd like you to cut off his resources. But not until the proper moment. Wait until I make the call."

"How long?" Sylian asks, clearly concerned now that money is involved. "Every day he wastes my funds."

"Not long," I assure him. "A day. Maybe two."

Sylian chews the inside of his cheek. "Fine. We can arrange that."

"He can't have access to anything. He needs to be cut off completely. No guns. No muscle. No money."

"Consider it done," Sylian says. He pauses, looking at me like I'm a strange animal in the woods. "You are sure you do not want to work for me?"

"I'm not sure I'd fit in," I tell him.

"I think you do not see yourself. Let me be your mirror."

He motions into the hallway. I follow him.

"You enjoy challenges. You trust no one. You can keep information to yourself but provide what's essential when necessary. You are strategic. And, it appears, loyal."

"I don't even know what you sell," I pretend.

"Do not play dumb with me," he laughs, rounding another corner. "Drugs and guns. Unless you know something I don't?"

"I don't know anything," I tell him. It's true, but not because I can't find out. I've chosen not to look too deeply into Sylian's dealings because I highly doubt his activities are limited to drugs and guns. There's a bigger weapons trade out there that can earn a person quite a bit more money. Money to afford a compound like this. Missiles.

Nuclear weapons. Materials to *build* those weapons. If he's involved in arms deals, I'd rather not know.

"Clever girl," Sylian smiles.

There's light up ahead. Sylian pushes the door open, revealing an outdoor space in the center of the compound. It's surrounded by walls, but it's massive. A giant tree grows in the center. On the horizon, rolling hills frame the sunset.

"We are no different than any other organization," he says with conviction. "All business done on a large scale comes with a cost."

"That's why it's up to each individual to decide what they can afford," I respond.

He smiles. "I see why Logan focused his attentions on you. You challenge something very fundamental in him. You have a piece he doesn't. You may beat him at his own game."

"I'm tired of feeling hunted. Of feeling like prey."

Sylian waves a hand in the air. "Predator, prey. None of that means anything."

"You don't think so?"

"No," he shakes his head. "The smallest bird hunts worms in the dirt. The worms eat the bacteria in the soil. And even the mightiest lion can destroyed by an infection of that same, tiny bacteria the worm ate yesterday." He pauses, looking at the sky. "Predator, prey. The idea is nonsense. It's not a pyramid out there." He raises a finger. Traces the outline of the setting sun. "Don't you see?"

I shake my head. "No."

"It's not a pyramid. It's a circle." He looks at me again. "We are *all* predators. We are *all* prey. When we live in balance, we survive, together. In this way, we need each other."

A strange feeling washes over me. For the first time in a

long time, I can imagine my life without Logan in it. I'm suddenly confident that I'll beat him. I'm going to win.

It's a circle.

"I appreciate the job offer, but I'm preoccupied," I tell him. Sylian nods. "But I know someone who might be an excellent replacement for Logan."

"Who?"

My promises have to be kept. I hate to do it, but Gabrielle only asked me for one thing. And even if I don't like it, who am I to judge her sense of justice?

"Her name is Gabrielle. She worked with Logan at C.E.R.N. She's another brilliant mind in the tech security space. He cost her a job, there. I'm sure she'd love to take his."

Sylian glances back at the horizon, thinking. "It's quite even, isn't it?"

"Yes."

"I like the symmetry of it. I'll have my people find her."

"I can give you her number—"

"Gabrielle. C.E.R.N. That's enough. Tell her she'll hear from us."

"Sylian?"

"Yes."

"Respectfully, I have to ask... why did you show me all of this?" I point over my shoulder, back at the compound.

"You didn't enjoy the tour?"

"No, I'm only wondering why you trust me."

There's a long pause. Then, Sylian bursts out laughing. For the first time, I notice two men behind him. They keep their distance, about two hundred yards away at all times. But they're listening to us. Both of them carry rifles. They echo his laughter, because they've heard everything.

"My darling, girl. I do *not* trust you. I trust *me*. And I trust survival instinct. If you told a soul about this place— where it was, or what we did— you'd be as good as dead the moment the words left your mouth."

The sound of Sylian's laughter rings in my ears as we head back toward the compound. Before the door closes behind me, I risk one more look back at the setting sun. The circle on the horizon. Predator. Prey. None of it means anything at all. Maybe what's important whether you're the predator or the prey. Maybe it doesn't matter if people have fangs. Or teeth that bite. Or tails that twitch.

Maybe what matters is simply knowing what each person is capable of, and what you're capable of in return. Understanding your strengths. Even Sylian forgets that the little bacteria— the one that lives on his paws, that sleeps with him at night— could be the one that makes his castle come crumbling down.

9

LOGAN

I *nside C.E.R.N.*

MY GUN IS ALREADY DRAWN when I emerge from the tunnels. A simple polyester mask covers my face, night vision goggles perched over the top.

It's pitch-black upstairs. I've cut the power to this section from down below. Two guards arrive, tasers in hand. C.E.R.N. is the kind of place that relies on first level security measures. They try to keep the bad guys out as their main line of defense, and give very little thought to what protocols should exist for when the bad guys have already accessed the space. Compared to the criminals I run with, these guards are mall cops.

A single shot takes out the first guard. The second feels his way through the darkness, flashlight in hand, bewildered. Even through the night vision goggles, I can see the shock registering on his face. Can smell his metallic concern sweating into the air.

Pop! Another bullet. Another guard down.

My legs pound down the hallway, passing door after door. The alarm is still ringing, but if I'm lucky, no one will have registered serious concern yet. Judging by the guard's surprise, this is likely the case. They'll think the pressure sensor was falsely triggered, or that the door came open due to faulty hardware. No one will leap to the conclusion C.E.R.N. has been invaded. Not yet. Not until they find the lifeless forms of the guards, still and silent on the tile floor.

Finally, I reach the elevator. The doors open. My finger hovers above the buttons. The first level is the most expedient route. But there might be more security by the exits. I gamble on a different choice and hit the button for the second floor. The elevator carries me upward, obedient. In no time at all, the doors open and I'm spilling out into the corridor.

On this level, big decisions are made. It's tailored to look more like a traditional office environment so the executives in charge of C.E.R.N. can be comfortable. My eyes scan the door numbers, looking for what I need. There. At the end of the hall. A simple sign on a brown door reads "ALICE."

The ALICE room is to C.E.R.N. what Huston is to NASA. It's their base of operations. The conference headquarters, where experiments are planned. It's where the fate of the large hadron collider is determined. In the Alice room, foreign diplomats argue over resources and debate the dangers of quantum experimentation. Fights are had, resolutions are found. And, because it serves as host to many important guests, the ALICE room has one other special quality: an emergency exit.

I open the door, closing it behind me. There's a table in the center of the room. To buy me time, I push it against the door at angle, turning it on its side beneath the handle to make it impossible to open.

The walls in the ALICE room are lined by bookshelves. The titles are all science related, both contemporary and ancient. My fingers scan the books, stopping when I find what I'm looking for. A dusty volume containing the works of Isaac Newton.

The cover creaks as I open it. Inside, there's not pages, but a tiny handheld tablet. This is the key to opening the emergency exit. Only a few people know the password, and it changes monthly. For anyone else, the time needed to crack the tablet would be too great to warrant trying in the need of escape.

But I've left myself a backdoor.

When I worked at C.E.R.N., I made sure I maintained permanent access to their security networks. Like a ghost, I've always been in the background, even after I left the organization behind to pursue greater endeavors.

The tablet starts up to a blank screen, requesting a username and password. I'll need to enter my master key. It's a blank I've programmed to exist behind what the powers-that-be at C.E.R.N. believe to be the main login credentials. The key may change frequently, and I'm sure they've erased it many times since I left, but the key they altered was never the master. The master is known only to me.

There's a pounding at the door. Voices echo from the other side. They must have discovered the guards, motionless downstairs. I don't have much time. A deep breath. I cross my fingers, hoping my master key hasn't been discovered. If it has, my exit will be... *messier* than anticipated.

A few quick taps and I'm in. The master key works. I open the main security panel on the tablet, and quickly locate the emergency exit in the ALICE room. As soon as it's activated on the tablet, one of the bookshelves pops away from the wall, revealing a separation.

My arms strain with the effort of pushing the bookshelf aside to clear the way. Hidden wheels lie beneath the bookshelf's bottom support, but it's still heavy, laden down with the weight of many pages. It's not an easy route, but in an emergency, it's better than nothing. When I've fully pushed the bookshelf aside, there's simple metal door left behind, serviced by an electronic deadbolt, which is controlled by the tablet and already set to the unlocked position.

The metal door opens with a squeal, revealing a set of steps. As I run up them, I hear the table in the ALICE room break into pieces. The guards have gained entry. They're right behind me.

My legs burn as I leap up the stairs, pushing on a hatch above my head and emerging into the cool, crisp night air. It bleeds into my lungs, making me feel alive and victorious.

I'm running across the fields that surround C.E.R.N., a black speck in the night, invisible and impossible to catch. When I reach my car, I glance over my shoulder, chest heaving. There's a few people at the emergency exit, but they're just dots against the landscape. I can feel their confusion from here. They're so very far away from understanding what's just happened. Undoubtedly, they'll search the place from top to bottom to try and ascertain what's been taken. Or maybe, what's been left behind. Bomb threats are a recurring issue at C.E.R.N. They'll surely sweep the place.

But they'll never know what I know. That the thing I've taken— the envelope in my pocket— was never theirs in the first place. C.E.R.N. is just a pawn in a game. A game Zoe thinks is hers, but that really belongs to me.

My seatbelt clicks into place and I rev the engine, taking one last look at that golden sphere on the horizon. In a way,

Zoe's done me a favor by giving me a chance to reflect on my past at C.E.R.N. I'm not sure what she expected me to learn from the puzzle she constructed— from Gabrielle, or my old workplace. But what it's taught me is that I'm unstoppable, and those who stand in my way always, *always* lose.

The sphere on the horizon glitters, winking at me like a golden, flickering sun. I think about Zoe, and how we're connected. Together, we make a circle, just like that sphere on the horizon. She starts where I end. She can never escape me.

The engine purrs as I press on the accelerator, enjoying the way it responds to my commands. The landscape is a blur in my rearview mirror, and I speed away from my past, clocking ninety miles per hour. Nothing but a shadow in the night. Just the way I like it.

WHEN I GET BACK to the safe house, I don't open the letter right away. Instead, I let it sit on the counter, ripening. Waiting. I don't want to open it until I know I have the upper hand. It's time to check on my minions.

A quick phone call connects me with Smith.

"Well?"

"Hey," Smith's voice crackles on the other end. The connection is bad. "Uh, what's up."

It takes everything I have not to throw my phone across the room. "Did you get them?"

"Here's the thing," Smith says, tentative. "It wasn't them."

A lump gathers in my throat. It's acidic, the burning by product of some unsettled feeling that's been brewing in my gut for a few days.

"What do you *mean* it wasn't them?"

"The people living in their house. They were doppel-gängers," Smith answers. "Pretty good lookalikes, too. About the same height and weight. Didn't know anything about this stuff."

"You mean to tell me," my voice is too calm. Controlled. "You've been following the wrong people this entire time?"

"Yeah," Smith says. "They said they rented the place off Craigslist. Told me it was a great deal. Listed for half of what it should have cost. The day they came to look at it, there was fifty other couples checking it out too. They were surprised they got it, because their credit isn't all that great. But the girl who rented it to them said they could have it if they agreed to send emails from a certain account, and make some phone calls from two cell phones they've left on the dresser."

"And they *agreed* to that?"

"It's Log Angeles," Smith says. "Rents are out of control. Have you seen the housing prices?"

"Thank you for the HGTV special," I spit, trying to plan my next move. "Hold them. See if you can extract more information."

"They don't know anything," Smith pushes back. "I let them go."

"You *let them go?*"

"Sylian wouldn't like it."

"Sylian does whatever's necessary for the job—"

"This isn't the job though, is it?" Smith says. "These people are nobodies. They're collateral damage. They disappear, it's more attention on us. And Sylian doesn't like it when we draw attention where we don't have to."

"You're making strategic decisions now?"

There's a long pause. Smith is far down on the organizational ladder. *Very* far down. He's walking a fine line.

"Just protecting my ass, that's all," he says. "Don't want you to pin a bad call on me."

"How about this? When I talk to Sylian, I'll let him know you can't follow directions."

Another pause. Smith doesn't have the direct line to Sylian that I do. He's met him, but he can't reach him at will. He has to rely on guys like me, and he eats shit for it.

"It was a mistake," he backtracks. "I shouldn't have let them go. We'll find them."

"Don't bother," I tell him, still seething. "Stay outside the house. Watch it. Make sure no one else comes inside. If somebody does, hold them. Try not to fuck it up again."

"Roger," Smith starts to say, but I cut him off before he can get the word out. The line goes dead.

Without my consent, my feet carry me across the room, stopping in front of the kitchen counter. There, Zoe's envelope sits. My hands reach for it, and I imagine how it would feel to drop it in the garbage disposal.

Instead, I open it up. I can't rely on Smith, so I'll have to find Zoe using my own skillset. Tonight will be a long night, dedicated to locating my prey. But first, the letter. The game. I unfold the page within, and begin to read.

~

"You've done so well,
   We'll let you know,
   Where your suitcase
   Had to go.
   Keep playing
   for more info, pretty,
   Your case resides
   In a major city.

But before you try
To guess which one
Finish our game
It's lots of fun.
Another clue awaits you
In the place from whence you came
*Keep your head on, even **Keil***
"Captain" means its name.
The spot is where you left her
The place is where she died
You took her pride and left her there
We wonder if you cried?
Pick one vial
not one more
Don't you trust
That fickle floor
All you need's within you
The liquid pain is there
Two choices are before you
Pick one that shows you care."

THE LATTER HALF of the poem appears to be instructions that won't make sense until I've reached the destination in question. But the first half— the first half I understand immediately.

Zoe has done her homework. She's dug up the body. She knows where it all began, for me. Two lines from the poem play on repeat in my ears.

*Keep your head on, even **keil***
"Captain" means its name.

The word "Keel" might looked misspelled to most, but

not to me. I know exactly what Zoe wants. She wants me to go to Keil, Germany. She wants me to go to my hometown.

I scan the poem again, noting the clue about where my suitcase might be.

Your case resides

In a major city.

Keil is not a major city by most definitions, although it's large for a coastal town. Still, it doesn't have the large population of a major metropolis. If my keepsakes are really in a major city, Keil is probably not the end location.

I'm pacing now, tracing a circle in the living room. I *could* try to find the case. Even if they claim the list of vaults is kept offline, it's hard for me to believe the bank *La Bismel* wouldn't keep virtual records of their international mini-vaults *somewhere.* I could try to find the list and skip Zoe's game, retrieving my suitcase on my own and then hunting her down. Or perhaps find records of their real estate holdings. They'd likely need to own the land to construct any kind of vault, even a small one. Then again, even if I *can* find the list, how many of their many vaults are likely to be located in a major city? All of them, most likely. No one wants to drive to the country side to retrieve a valuable item. The clue isn't broad enough.

I still need to play Zoe's game.

I may not be able to find my keepsakes— *yet*— but that doesn't stop me from finding Zoe and Mike. She thinks a couple doppelgängers are enough to keep off her trail? Please.

My fingers stretch. I flex out the tension, then open up my laptop and rest them on the keyboard, preparing to do what I do best.

Zoe can hide. But she can't run. Not from me.

10

ZOE

D*ubrovnik, Croatia.*

I'M STAYING with an older couple on the outskirts of Dubrovnik. Cassandra's arranged for them to house me in exchange for more money than they make in a year. As part of the transaction, they agreed not to ask me any questions about what I'm doing here.

The house is a small, three room building in a Croatian village. The word "village" sounded picturesque when I first heard it, but now that I'm here, the image doesn't match up to reality. There's no quaint cobblestone streets. No thatched roods. Just miles of farmland and open space, dying grass and weathered trees in-between. Each house is at least a mile away from the next, creating an uncomfortable sense of isolation.

The older couple that houses me— a husband and wife — didn't say a word when Sylian's men dropped me off. I left the car in Dubrovnik. There's another one, parked just outside the chicken coop, that was waiting for me when I arrived. I told Cassandra changing vehicles so often was excessive, but she insisted Logan has access to satellites and could trace the license plate if a traffic camera happened to ID my face. I think it's unlikely, but then again, it's better to be safe than sorry. Cassandra might be eccentric, but she's not stupid.

The couple doesn't tell me their names. Still, I feel close to them. The wife makes me breakfast in the morning, seating me on a couch in the living room. The husband leans back in his recliner, eating his eggs and watching something on the decade old TV in the corner. It's the news.

At first, I don't pay any attention. But then, I see an image of a familiar golden dome. It's a spherical building. The exterior of C.E.R.N. The eggs I'm eating fall off my fork. My chest tightens.

"Can you turn it up?" I ask the husband. He stares at me, shocked I've spoken. He shakes his head, confused. Suddenly, I realize Cassandra's arrangement isn't the only reason for their silence. He doesn't speak English.

The husband motions at the kitchen, beckoning his wife. She enters the living room, wiping her hands on her apron.

"The TV," I say. "Louder?"

She nods, grabbing the remote. A news anchor on the television reports in Croation.

"*Sinoć su ubijena dva stražara—*"

"English?" I ask her, desperate to know what's happened.

"Eh," she looks are her husband for help. He doesn't offer any. "Killed," she says, nodding at a picture on the screen. There's an image of two guards, wearing crisp white shirts. It looks like photos off their employee badges. She drags a hand across her throat to emphasize the point.

My stomach turns. I'm not hungry anymore. The plate squeaks as I push it away from me, running out the front door. My feet are in control, taking me past the chicken coop into the field behind the house. Tall grass waves around my knees. I sink into the dirt, the truth of what's happened making my skin prickle.

I got those men killed. They died because of me.

My breakfast comes up in a waves, and before I know what's happening, I'm vomiting into the grass. My arms shudder, and the ground beneath me seems to open up, inviting me to disappear. Everything spins. It's like I'm suddenly aware of the Earth's rotation.

I am the reason they're dead.

I'm not a person who scares easily. Not one prone to panic. But in the rare moments the world crashes down on me, there's only one person who can fix it. My fingers shake as I pull my burner phone out of my pocket and call Mike.

He answers on the first ring. "Zoe?" His voice is concerned. I'm not calling at my usual time. He knows something's wrong. "What's wrong?"

"I can't do it," I'm crying. "Those men died because of me."

"What men?" Mike asks, sounding a little frantic. "Are you hurt? Are you okay?"

"He killed two guards at C.E.R.N.," I explain, desperate for Mike to understand. "Those men had families. They were somebody's husband. Somebody's son. They died because of me."

"They didn't die because of you," Mike says, voice soft. "They died because of Logan."

His words don't help. He's not making me feel better. And Mike *always* makes me feel better.

"Zoe?" Mike's voice sounds so far away. I don't answer.

Everything is still spinning. "*Zoe*," Mike says again. "I need you to calm down. Tell me what's around you."

"A house," I say, vague.

"Be specific. What kind of house?"

"A blue one."

"Is it big or small?"

"Small."

"How many trees are outside?"

I count. "Five."

"Are they a species you know?"

"Maybe Oak."

"How many clouds are in the sky?"

"Seven."

"Are you sitting or standing?"

"Sitting."

"Do you feel the ground underneath you?"

"Yes."

"What's it like?"

The dirt gives beneath my fingers. For the first time, I notice it's damp. "A little wet, actually," I tell him.

He laughs. "Hope you brought other clothes."

"This is my last pair of pants," I tell him. "I probably smell."

"You could never," he lies to me. "Feel better?"

"A little."

"Now that you're back with me, I want to tell you how you're different than him."

"I can't—"

"Let me finish."

"I'm not gonna blow smoke up your ass and lie and say you're nothing like him, because there's things you have in common. It's true, Zoe. He wouldn't have picked you otherwise."

My fingers close around a blade of grass near my shoes, splitting it into pieces.

"You still with me?" Mike asks on the other end. "Don't quit on me yet." He knows what I'm thinking. Knows I want to hang up on him right now. This is something I hate about being married. How the other person gets to see so much of you. Gets to know you so well, inside and out. It's a fact that makes it hard to escape getting called on your bullshit.

"Still here," I say through gritted teeth.

"Good," he answers. "Because now we're at the important part. The way you're different."

There's a buzz in the background. The timer Mike sets with every call. It's gone off. We're past two minutes.

"We should hang up," I tell him. "It's fine. I'm okay."

"Forget the timer," he says.

"But—"

"It doesn't matter. I need to say this. You and Logan share some traits in common, but the thing that sets you apart is the most important quality of all. People aren't really defined by their personality traits. Being aloof, or liking a certain TV show, or your favorite dessert... none of that really makes you who you *are*."

"It doesn't?"

"No," Mike says. "Because that stuff changes over time. People change. Preferences shift. But what makes you who you are is something *else*. It's that inner compass. Your center. I don't like new agey stuff, but—"

"But?"

"It's you *soul*. Your central self that determines who you are. Not the preferences, but the place they come from. It's the part of you that made you so upset this morning over something that wasn't even your fault. It's your *core*. And

Zoe," Mike pauses. "Your core is the best one I've ever fucking met in my life."

"Really?"

"Yes," he says. "Your core is good. You care about other people. About what happens to them. You cared so much about me you walked across a national park to find me. You're not a victim like Logan. You're a hero. You might have some traits in common, but you use yours to help others. He uses his to help himself, at the *expense* of others. Don't you see? That's why he picked you."

Mike's words ring in my ears. I've been so busy trying to stay two steps ahead of Logan that I never stopped to wonder why he chose *me* in the first place.

"You represent what Logan *could* be," Mike continues. "If he had a better center. If he were stronger. He can never rise to your level. So he's got to try to pull you down to his."

"I love you," I tell Mike.

"Come home," he says. "When you're finished. I need you back in one piece."

I want to promise him it'll happen, but I don't make promises I can't keep.

11

LOGAN

G*eneva, Safe House.*

I'VE BEEN SCOURING the dark web for hours, seeking Zoe's footprint. I've been at it so long that time has no meaning anymore. The room is dim, except for light from my computer screen. Blackout curtains cover the safe house windows, ensuring I'm not interrupted. I'm wholly enveloped in the world that exists within my computer. Beside me, a half-eaten take out meal begins to wilt. It's from a restaurant two blocks away that delivers.

I will find you, Zoe.

Ordinary people don't know this, but computers aren't just machines meant to make daily life easier. No, computers are more than that. Computers are portals. Portals to an entire digital world within.

It's a virtual world, but it's one we all live in whether we know it or not. Everything we do relies on technology. Credit card transactions. Cell phone calls. Banal tasks in our daily lives leave traces behind on the internet. This information is accessible from the dark web— the internet *behind* the internet. It's a place for criminals, intelligence offers, and anyone who wants to find someone else.

The dark web accounts for over 80% of the actual internet, and yet most people never access it. These pages aren't indexed by search engines like Google. They won't appear in your queries. But they're there, filled with countless tools. Countless resources. A million ways to make trouble.

I've hidden my IP address behind a VPN. A virtual private network, paid for by my employer. Most of our transactions involve the dark web. It's the perfect place to conduct an arms deal. Still, the VPN only offers so much security. To further obscure my identity, I've layered multiple proxy IPs on top of one other. Every keystroke travels first to India, then to South America, then to a hundred other locations before reaching my end receiver. It's an excellent way to cloak my location in case someone decides to work backward, tracing the IP address.

So far, I've searched both Zoe and Mike's credit card transactions. They're all located in Silverlake. Clearly, these were conducted by the doppelgängers she hired. Zoe's too smart to use a card near her present location. Same goes for their cell phones. But then again... would Zoe *really* allow herself to fall out of touch with the people she cares about? No, I decide. It's anathema to who she is.

She must be using a burner phone.

This complicates things. A burner phone won't be tied to Zoe's identity, so I'll have to search using some other characteristic. My stomach churns. Finding Zoe will require me to do something very dangerous.

I have to access the NSA's metadata.

People like me aren't the only ones interested in

accessing phone calls across the world. The NSA has been contracting with cell phone companies for years, storing all cell phone calls as metadata in quantities the human mind cannot comprehend. There's safety, in collecting trillions of gigabytes of information. The sheer quantity of calls recorded creates a type of anonymity. The NSA is interested in catching terrorists, not intruding on the personal or private moments of ordinary citizens.

But still, the information is there.

I've only accessed the NSA's servers once before. It was at Sylian's request. He needed to find the location of a competitor selling arms on his territory. I did everything in my power to cloak my identity. Assured Sylian the NSA wouldn't even sense the breach. Wouldn't know we were there. I was arrogant. Too sure of myself.

Within a few moments of my entering the system, Sylian received a call. I'll never forget the way the blood drained from his face. He said very little over the phone, but when the call was over, he told me we were never to try to access their servers again.

Sylian's competitor disappeared a few weeks later, without any intervention from us. When I asked Sylian how he had the seller taken care of, Sylian responded, "I didn't have to. They were already watching him. He broke the rules, and now he's gone. Always remember that, Logan. There are rules. Even for us. They watch." I never found out who "they" were.

My fingers hover above the keyboard, waiting for instruction. I'm frozen, wondering if this is really worth it. Then, I think about what Zoe's done to me. The roses on the floor. The red and blue wires. The ghosts from my past.

My fingers leap to life. I start the hack.

Accessing their servers isn't hard. I've done it before.

Already laid the groundwork. Already made the map. Within an hour, I'm back inside.

Because the metadata covers trillions of phone calls, I'll need to search using specific qualities. Name and social security number won't work, as this is a burner phone. Of course, the NSA is equipped to deal with that. Terrorists don't usually purchase cell phones with their legal names.

I'll have to search by voice.

A quick stop to Instagram, and I find a video of Zoe and Mike at their wedding. It's not from Zoe's account. She doesn't have her own social media anymore. It's from an account belonging to her maid of honor, Tori. It's a short clip, sitting there on her stories, labeled "FRIENDS." In the video, Zoe is in her wedding dress, smiling. She's getting her makeup done. Tori puts the camera in her face. Says "How does it feel the be a bride?"

Zoe's eyes widen as she looks deep into the camera.

Speak, I think. *Just say a few words. It's all I need.*

There's a long pause, then, Zoe says, "It feels like I'm right where I'm supposed to be."

Got you, I smile. I grab the snippet and cut it into a loop, replaying her words over and over.

"Supposed to be, Supposed to be, Supposed to be..." Her voice echoes from my computer in waves. After awhile, it's as if she's in the room with me, a siren calling me closer.

In the NSA main-frame, there's a bar for search options. It's a shockingly simple interface they've created. Oddly user-friendly, considering what it hides.

I type in SEARCH: "Voice." MATCH: Quality / Tone / Gender / Pitch.

I've started with the most restrictive filters. If I don't get enough results, I'll broaden the field. But given the enormous amount of information, I'm expecting a narrow search is the best way to start.

My lungs expand as I inhale, pinning all my hopes on this moment. Then, I hit "enter."

Letters appear on the screen in a flurry, each of them outlining a different source file. Now, I just have to hope Zoe's made a long call to someone in the last week. The server only stores substantial calls longer than two minutes. No quick hellos. No accidental butt dials. The system was designed to outsmart terrorists, who need more than a few seconds to organize large operations.

The search finishes. There's five hundred thousand potential matches.

Zoe's voice isn't unique.

I begin the sorting process, eliminating by locale. I get rid of any calls where the language tag isn't "English." As far as I know, Zoe doesn't speak anything else. This cuts the number by more than half, bringing me down to the 200,000 range.

A quick scan of the filter options shows me one I haven't tried. "A.I.B.M.," which stands for "Artificial Intelligence Best Match." Leave it to the robots to accomplish what humans can't. When I turn the function on, the computer narrows potential matches down to a little over 1,500.

This is more manageable. There's nothing left to do now but sort. One by one, I click through the calls, listening to a brief sample. Sometimes, it's easy to eliminate a given file. A girl in high school calling her Mom? Delete. A man? Delete. One by one, the playing field narrows.

And then I hear it. Zoe's voice. "*They died because of me.*" It's followed by an answer. "*They died because of Logan.*"

Zoe and Mike are talking about me. My heart races. It's

satisfying, knowing I'm still the center of their world. Knowing that they can't escape me.

If they're calling each other, they aren't together. This makes sense. After what happened in Yosemite, of course Zoe would choose to split up. The strategy allows her to double her odds of success and avoid roping Mike into her situation. It's very noble. Very... *her.*

A quick click lets me flag the file and examine it for more details. I scroll through useless information like cell phone provider and the model of the phone, landing on what I'm really looking for: the location of the cell tower for both sender and recipient.

Clear as day, the treasure I've been seeking glitters on the screen.

CALLER: **Dubrovnik, Croatia.**

RECIPIENT: **Napa Valley, California, United States.**

Below each locale, coordinates provide an exact location for both, down to a few feet in accuracy.

Zoe is in Europe, and Mike is in Napa Valley.

I'll admit, I wasn't expecting to get two locations for the price of one. My knuckles crack as I close my laptop and reach for my phone. The hard work is over. Now it's time to have a little fun.

12

ZOE

*O*utside Dubrovnik, Croatia.

I'M WALKING ALONG A CREEK, dipping my toes in the water.

The wife, whose name I've learned is "Lucija," took me by the hand when I reached the house. She could see I was upset. She gave me a pastry she called a *kroštule*— a warm and flaky dessert baked in her own oven. Now, she's showing me the creek beyond the field that grows behind their house. We walk in silence, but every now and then, she'll point out a fish in the water. "*Izgled*," she points. "Look."

"It's nice," I tell her, watching a brown fish swim between the rocks. "Thank you," I say. She nods.

Just then, a ringing sound from my pocket. It's the burner phone.

Mike, I think. But when I answer, it's not him.

"He knows where you are," Sylian's voice surprises me on the other line.

"How?" My breath quickens.

"Let's just say he broke a promise he made me," Sylian answers. "Some friends at the NSA aren't happy with me."

"You have friends at the NSA?"

"Anyone who sells in a territory they're watching doesn't sell for very long. It's necessary, to make friends." Sylian answers. "This complicates everything. I've assured my friends Logan will be taken care of. If you don't finish him, I will."

"I can do it," I tell him.

"I'll be watching," he says. "In the meantime, you need to leave."

"I can't—"

"Logan accessed a call between you and Mike. He knows where both of you are."

"I have to tell Mike," I start to say, but Sylian cuts me off.

"I'm on it. Logan sent one of my men after him, but I've already redirected him. Mike is fine. But the house you're in—"

"What?"

"I have keystroke records through our VPN. My tech tells me he accessed the only gas line that runs through the village. The entire system is controlled by computers. Remember the colonial pipeline attack?"

The term triggers some vague recognition of news stories, played out late at night at a time when my life was normal. "Russian hackers?" I ask.

"They froze the pipeline, demanded payment to restart operations," Sylian confirms.

"You think Logan's going to hold gas hostage?" It's hard to hide my skepticism.

"No, I don't think that's what he'll do. If you can turn it off, you can also turn it *up*. One of our drones has already been deployed from the stash. I can't stop it."

There's a long pause as I realize what Sylian is saying.

"Zoe?" His voice echoes from the other line. "Zoe, are you there?"

"Thank you," I tell him. I'm about to hang up, but there's one more thing I have to do. "Sylian?"

"Yes."

"Remember how I said I'd let you know when it's time to pull the plug on Logan?"

"I've been waiting," he says, a smile in his voice.

"Do it," I tell him before hanging up.

Lucija looks at me, eyes wide. She knows something's wrong. I grab her arm.

"What's your husband's name?"

"Andre," she tells me, fear making the word exit her mouth in a flurry.

"Stay here," I say. She nods, and I leave her behind as I run back up the hill, moving as fast as my legs will carry me.

"Andre!" I shout, waving my arms. He's outside the house, a watering can in hand. "*Andre!*" He turns around, notices me running toward him. Concern is etched on his face. He peers down the valley toward the creek. He's worried something has happened to his wife.

When I reach him, I push open the side door to the house and stick my head inside. The unmistakable smell of gas fills my nose. Andre stands behind me. He shakes his head when he smells the gas. He starts to enter— to try and fix the source of the leak— but I put a hand on his shoulder. I tug on the end of my ear, asking him to listen. He does.

There's a hissing sound from the kitchen, from the fire-place. It's as if the pipes have filled with pressure and can't stand a single ounce more. Andre stares at me in horror, realizing there's no way to stop the leak when it's coming in from multiple points.

"It's going to explode," I tell him.

He seems to understand me, because he tries to run back inside to grab their valuables. "There's no time," I say, holding him back as best I can. He's much bigger than me, but sheer will power helps me keep him near the door.

Just then, a clicking noise echoes from overhead. We step outside, spotting the source of the sound. A drone, hovering just twenty feet overhead. There's a camera attached to it. It looks like a GoPro.

Logan is watching us, I think. *He wants to know if I live or die.*

Ignoring the drone, I pullAndre away from the house as fast I can, determination driving me forward. We've barely cleared the back gate when the explosion happens.

Boom. There's an enormous rattling from within the house. Bricks crumble from the chimney. Glass windows shatter. We dive to the ground, covering the back of our heads. Andre looks like he's been punched, and in some way, he has. His cough tells me the wind has been knocked out of him.

There's a silence in which I think the worst is over, but then... another explosion. This one is louder. Flames consume what once was the kitchen area, devouring the home in a ferocious rage.

The pilot light, I cringe, wishing I'd dared to turn it off.

Andre pulls his knees to his chest, in shock. He has the dazed look of a man unable to believe his entire life has been turned upside down in a single moment. A man who is suddenly faced with the terrible realization that every castle we built, is only built on sand.

The drone hovers lower, closing in on Andre like it enjoys watching his pain. Like it wants to record every second to savor later.

For a moment, the drone becomes Logan, his eyes laughing at me. Arms reaching for me.

Before I know it, I'm standing on top of the fence, a fallen brick in hand. I chuck it as hard as I can and the drone falls to the Earth with a sad, sweeping sound.

I walk toward it and pick it up, breaking off its wings in the process. The camera shakes as I pluck it from the drone's surface.

The lens stares at me, and I can feel Logan on the other end, watching. I smile at him.

"Enjoy this moment," I tell him. "Because the game's not over."

With that, I smash the camera lens into pieces, watching the shards fall onto the dirt. My fingers shake as I cover it with soil, burying the camera underground so deep I'm sure it can never be resurrected.

13

LOGAN

*S*afe House, Geneva.

Iт's as if I've seen her in person. Zoe's eyes, not so different in shape from mine, staring at me through the drone camera. It's been so long since I looked at her. So long since I observed her, taking in the minutiae of her movements. Noticed the way she scratches her temple when she's thinking. Watched the care with which she tucks her hair behind her ear.

There's something different about her, I think to myself. She seems more worldly than when I met her two years ago. More centered in herself. Maybe it's me she has to thank for that. Maybe I *have* changed in her some way after all, even if not in the way I intended.

She's right. The game isn't finished. I knew the gas explosion wouldn't kill her. If I'd wanted to kill Zoe, I would have dipped into our weapons supplies and launched an armed missile attack on the house. Sylian trusts me completely. I would have told him it was necessary in establishing cyber security. I'm excellent at creating elaborate stories and falsifying information to support my claims. If I'd wanted to, I would have convinced Sylian secret servers were hiding in the house's basement, attacking our firewalls. I could have made him believe the use of force was justified, and taken Zoe out with the stroke of a key.

Yes, it was in my power to kill her, but I didn't. I knew the gas would build pressure slowly. Zoe is the kind of person who notices trouble. I knew the second she smelled gas in the house, she'd evacuate herself and every one in it. Because that's what good prey does. It runs at the first sign of danger.

But then again, prey doesn't fight back. That's what makes Zoe interesting to me. She dares to fight those who are bigger and stronger. She is a mouse who thinks she is a wolf. Perhaps, if she had agreed to live a life with me, she would have evolved into a wolf under my care and encouragement.

But now, she'll always be a mouse.

The blackout curtains on the safe house window are still closed. Under the dim glow of my computer screen, I pack for Kiel. My hometown. The place where I left myself behind.

Zoe is correct. The game is not over. Not yet. When it ends, only one of us will be left standing. I'll make sure of it. I will let her die slowly. Let her realize what she's lost.

But not before I've had my fun.

14

ZOE

*O*utside Dubrovnik, Croatia.

MY SHOES STICK to the ground as I usher Lucija and Andre South across the creek-bed. It's raining, now. Just a gentle drizzle, but the raindrops feel like knives against my skin. My senses are on high alert. Every caw of a bird sounds like a warning. Every broken twig beneath my feet a cause for alarm.

We stay low under the cover of trees, letting their branches provide cover. There could be another drone out there, watching us. Or maybe the next drone will be armed with more than a camera. Either way, it's best to stay out of sight.

The nearest house is a fifteen minute drive away. On foot, it takes us an hour. The neighbor's home is a thatch-roofed cottage. It's quainter than the farm that Lucija and Andre manage, boasting far less square footage. Still, when the neighbor opens the door, she ushers us in without a question. In no time at all, we're sitting in her living room, cups of coffee in hand.

Lucija explains the entire scenario, talking a hundred miles a minute in Croatian, a language I don't speak. I know she's talking about the explosion by the way her hands move in the air, demonstrating the house expanding. Beside her, Andre sits as still as a statue, silent and haunted.

When I'm able to politely excuse myself, I find a quiet spot in the cottage's side yard. Sitting on the brick retaining wall, I call Mike, praying for an answer.

He doesn't pick up until the third ring.

"I'm okay," he says, skipping the hello. "Smith got me."

"Who?" I ask, alarmed.

"It's a long story," Mike sighs. "This Sylian character is really something. Interesting friend you've made."

"He offered to employ me," I tease. "Should I take him up on it?"

"I mean, this town car is the kind of ride I could get used to," Mike laughs.

"You left the house in Napa? But we agreed—"

"He knows where it is, Zoe," Mike answers. "It's not safe anymore. Sylian's guys say they have safe houses all over the world. They've offered me one. I'm going to take it."

My skin prickles. I hate that Mike has made this decision on his own. "We haven't talked about it."

"This is what I'm doing," Mike says, cutting me off. I know what he's thinking. I have no right to insist on making every decision together when I left unilaterally. Still, it stings.

"This Smith guy, he's a tradesperson like me. He really hates Logan," Mike continues. "I trust him."

"You're a carpenter. He's an assassin. I wouldn't say he's a tradesperson. You're sure you trust him?"

Mike doesn't answer. Smith must be listening.

"Where's the safe house?" I ask.

"Los Angeles," Mike says. "I asked them to put me close to the final trap. There's been some issues with the building. One of the doors isn't firing."

"Let Richard handle it," I say, referencing one of Mike's best employees.

"I need to see it for myself. Need to know it works. You were right, Zoe. If you're the one who's gonna be in there, the trap has to be built by me. It's destiny."

He's used an argument I can't negate. I hate when he uses my own weapons against me.

"Be safe," I tell him. "Don't trust anyone."

"Don't worry," Mike answers, the tone of his voice telling me he's not so sold on Smith after all. "Even golden retrievers bite."

The reference makes me smile. Mike tells me he loves me, and then the line goes dead.

My eyes scan the night sky for stars, and find a hundred more than I'm used to. There's so little ambient light out here in the country side that you can see every pinprick in the sky.

It starts to rain again, and even though it's only a drizzle, I can feel a storm brewing. The cottage is so small, it's necessary to stand outside for privacy. If I want to make another call, now might be my only chance.

I pound the number into my cell phone, hating to do it. We arranged everything in advance so I wouldn't have to call her unless there was an emergency, but now, I need her.

"Cassandra?" I ask when the line comes alive.

"Zoe!" She exclaims, happy to hear from me. "Your parents love the island. Our goal is to replace all past trauma with good experiences. Your Mom is learning to jet ski. Can you believe it?"

"That nice," I say, rolling my eyes. What a lovely holiday.

"I'm hoping if they love it they'll move here. Can you believe it? Wouldn't that be great? And if *they* move here, maybe you and Mike could move here too!"

The idea makes my blood run cold. Despite all odds, Cassandra and I have formed some kind of friendship. But I never forget that she once stalked Mike. She was obsessed with him after their relationship ended, unable to let him go. She claims she's finally developed past the preoccupation, but I've noticed that she can't help but slip his name into conversation. Every now and then, she'll ask how he's doing. There's a sense of urgency in her questions that makes me think she hasn't totally given up on him, and that she never really will.

Still, she's become my unlikely benefactor. She has the money we need to make this operation a reality, and the personal grudge against Logan to want to invest.

"That's great," I tell her. "But I have to survive this experience first."

"What happened?" She sounds concerned. In some ways, Cassandra is a more genuine friend than others I've gained over the years. She can't help but be exactly who she is in any given moment, so I always know her concern for me is real.

"Logan blew up the house I was staying at," I tell her. A gasp from the other line. "This husband and wife, it's so wrong, so unfair to them. They didn't do anything to deserve this except help me."

"Don't worry about a thing," Cassandra says, suddenly all business. "I'll take care of them. And you. We need to move you right away."

"Thank you," I tell her.

"I'll have a car there in an hour. Germany is up next, right?"

My body trembles a little, but I'm not sure it's the cold. The next stop on my itinerary is the place where Logan became a man. The place where he became a predator.

"Germany," I confirm. Part of me wishes I could stop now. Could turn around and go back. But we've come too far. If I don't seek answers now, I might not ever get them.

15

LOGAN

E *dge of the Black Forest, Germany.*

I'M HALFWAY through Germany when the blackout happens. The ride in the town car has been seamless, up until now. Ordinary. One driver and an armed guard in the front, with me, alone, in the back. The level of luxury accommodation I'm accustomed to.

We're North of Freiburg but West of Stuttgart when my laptop locks me out. I'm using a wireless hotspot, checking on my accommodations in Keil when it suddenly asks me to re-enter my credentials. I do. But the system denies me access.

That's when I know I'm in trouble.

It's a blackout, I think. The term "blackout" is what other people might call "being fired." But in my business, it means losing access to your systems, bank accounts, and maybe even your life.

How could Sylian be unhappy with my work? I've provided him with top grade technical support, making the impossible possible. With my help, he's securely transferred weapons around the world, safeguarding funds and handling major transactions without outside interference. I've protected him. Given him my best.

He'll never find anyone better. This I'm sure of.

My mind races, cataloging my personal accounts and resources. I'll lose access to many of the perks of my position. Weaponry. Thugs on call. Easy transportation and global safe houses. But luckily, many of these things can be purchased. I've been handsomely compensated over the years, and have even managed to siphon away some of Sylian's funds under the guise of false expenses that never happened. That money sits in a Swiss bank account, untouchable by anyone except me. I can buy the luxury experience that working for Sylian provides. I'm independently wealthy. I don't need him.

Just then, the car slows down. We're pulling over. When I try the handle, it doesn't budge. The door is locked. Patiently, I wait. There's a gun in my bag, and I pull it out, keeping my finger on the trigger.

The driver opens the door. "Get out," he says. I do.

The driver motions to the armed guard. The guard exits the passenger side and stands beside him, unbuttoning his coat.

"Sylian wants you to know it's all business," the driver says. "Nothing personal."

The armed guard holds up a screen. There, a live video call plays. Sylian's face appears.

"Old friend," Sylian says. "It has to be this way."

"I didn't know you were unhappy," I tell him.

"Your work is impeccable," Sylian nods. "But my informant tells me you've been using our resources for your own... shall I say, pet project?"

He knows about Zoe.

"We all make mistakes," I answer.

"Not with my money." Sylian smiles. Nods at a tech offscreen. "I'd like you to meet your replacement," he says.

The view widens as the tech patches in another remote caller. Her video appears, and my breath catches in my throat.

Gabrielle.

"You took more than a job from me, Logan," Gabrielle smiles. "I can only hope this is just the start of us, how do the Americans say?" She pauses. "Ah, yes. 'Getting *even*.'"

Acid churns in my stomach. Zoe is trying to teach me something. Trying to erase history and reverse the past. It's a game of cosmic tag.

"Goodbye, Logan," Sylian says. The screen goes black.

The armed guard closes the computer and reaches into his pocket, but I'm too fast for him. My gun is already in my hand, and I let the bullets fly. They discharge in a spray, and I must be more nervous than I realize, because before I know it, I've emptied the entire clip. Six shots. The guard crumples to the ground in a heap.

"Tell Sylian that sure as fuck felt personal," I say. But the driver doesn't answer. He's already reaching for the gun the guard dropped as he fell. I don't have time to reload. Instead, I take off into the trees beside me.

Growing up in Germany means at least I know exactly where I am. The Black Forest is home to dense evergreen trees. It's a place shrouded in mystery. The place where the Brothers Grimm Fairytales originated. As I race into the darkness, I think about my own fairytale ending and what it would look like, if I could have it.

In my fairytale ending, I'm a giant and Zoe is a princess. I crush her into a bloody mess beneath my shoe.

*O*utskirts of Dubrovnik, Croatia.

CASSANDRA KEEPS HER WORD. Before the night is over, a car appears to take me to the airport. A woman and two men unload from within. The woman looks fashionable. Wealthy. She's holding a black portfolio in her hands.

She barely acknowledges me, but goes straight toward Andre and Lucija, speaking in Croatian. She snaps at the man beside her and opens the portfolio, showing Lucija and Andre pictures of massive estates.

Their mouths drop open. They're embracing each other like they've just won the lottery.

That's when I realize: Cassandra is going to rebuild their house. She's not only going to rebuild it, but give the something better than what they had.

Say what you want about Cassandra, I think, *But she's putting her money to good use.*

A driver motions to me from outside the front door. He

points at his watch. Time to get moving. I'd like to leave without much fanfare. I grab what's left of my things— the backpack I was carrying when the house exploded— and head for the door. I can't help but pause at the frame, looking over my shoulder.

Andre and his neighbor are deeply involved with the designer, talking plans, pointing at pictures. But Lucija notices me. Looks up. She smiles, saying everything words can't. Things are right between us. She winks at me, and I take that as my cue to sneak away.

Cool air hits my lungs. The night is crisp and even. The driver opens the door for me, and in no time at all we're speeding along a dark Croatian road. There's nothing but farmland for miles. Every now and then, I peer upward, scanning the horizon for any sign of a drone. None appears.

We reach the airport, and it's even smaller than the one that first welcomed me to Europe. There's no hangars. There's no massive jets. Just a single dirt runway, and a few small planes. These are ultralight aircraft— tiny planes that remind of the kind the Wright Brothers invented. They're all wings, with little in the way of seats. Two people is all they'll hold. But for tonight, two is enough.

The driver opens my door for me. He's holding a black case. When he passes it to me, I unzip it, finding another American passport displaying a false identity.

"Georgia Winthrop," I read the name aloud.

"Miss Cassandra worried your documents had been destroyed," the driver answers. He waves down the pilot. The two men talk for a minute, again in Croatian. They shake hands. The driver motions for me to approach.

He gives me a lift toward the plane's door, and the pilot buckles me in the backseat. He puts headphones over my ears, and soon we're soaring into the distance, heading toward Germany.

When I peer out the window, a thousand pinpricks of light stare back at me from down below. They belong to houses. To shops. To countless people living their everyday lives, unaware that people like Logan move among us, ready to disrupt our lives at any opportunity.

I used to be one of those people.

The thought makes my stomach churn. Suddenly, the lights below remind me of stars, and I wonder if I'm upside down, flying in reverse. It's a strange feeling, forgetting which way is up. For the rest of the flight, I close my eyes, trying to find my bearings within myself.

WHEN WE LAND IN GERMANY, it's still nighttime. Disembarking is less of a hassle in a small plane, and in no time at all, I'm in another town car. It takes me down the coast, on the edge of the baltic sea. Waves crash against the rocks, their arcs large and imposing, pitch black in the night.

The city of Kiel reveals itself in long bridges and pastel houses. It may technically be a city, but not a big one. A sign on the outskirts lists the population at two-hundred-and-fifty-thousand.

We curve around another bend and stop in front of a small, white house in the city's center. It's not much to look at.

When I step out of the car, the driver waits for me, headlights still on. I wave him away, giving him the signal to leave. He rolls down the passenger window. Looks at me with his eyebrows raised.

"You're sure?"

"Yes," I nod.

He shrugs and takes off. At the end of the day, I'm a job for him. In his mind, it's my funeral.

A porch light clicks on as I step toward the house. It's painted in one color. The exterior and the trim blend together in the same shade of pale cream. Something about the effect is unsettling. It's like the house is trying to disappear.

The front steps creak where the wood has thinned. The termites are making good work of the banisters. Overgrown shrubs reach over the porch, their branches like tentacles threatening to consume unwelcome visitors. There's no doorbell. Just an old-fashioned actual bell attached to the frame. It hangs down in a swoop, the gold exterior now faded to bronze.

I ring it. The door opens.

"*Du bist hier*," the woman on the other side of the doorway says to me. "I did not think you'd come."

"People keep saying that to me," I smile at her. "It's making me question my choices."

There's a moment where neither one of us speaks to the other. I wonder if she's going to turn me away.

"Ingrid," I say, her name heavy, like metal in my mouth. "Aren't you going to invite me in?"

She looks me up and down, still thinking. Then, she shrugs.

"Come in," she waves me inside, and I can't help but look away when she locks eyes with me. Her eyes are so familiar. They're just like Logan's. The same watery shade. Same shape. I shouldn't be surprised.

After all, she is his Mother.

17

LOGAN

The Black Forest, Germany.

THE TREES ARE dark and dense, but I'm not afraid. This forest was made for creatures like me. Creatures who prefer to operate in the shadows.

Branches snap as I make my way deeper into the darkness, staying far enough away that the driver can't hear me, but close enough that I can keep my eyes on him.

He's on his cellphone. He hasn't entered the forest because of the legends. The stories. Locals know the Black Forest is filled with dark spirits. Children grow up hearing tales of disappearances. Of strange animals that are neither beast nor bird, ready to snap you up from the crib and raise you as their own. It's a place locals are taught to stay away from.

There's no doubt the driver is on the phone with Sylian right now, explaining what has happened. Once Sylian finds out the guard is dead, he'll let the driver abandon his post. That's one thing about Sylian: he doesn't expect people to step outside of their roles within his organization. Drivers *drive*. Muscle is *muscle*. If one person fails, he doesn't expect someone else to step up and cover for them. It's a strategy that enables him to employ idiots like Smith. Another reason an innovator like me could never be happy there.

I'm glad to be set free. He's done me a favor, really.

The car's headlights turn on. My legs burn as I crouch down, peering around the tree trunk that obscure my form. Tires screech as the driver pulls away from the scene, plunging the road back into complete and total darkness.

Once I'm sure he's gone, I emerge from my hiding spot, heading back toward the road. Staying close to the road has its risks. I hate to be so exposed, so out in the open, and would prefer to stay in the forest. I'm not afraid to spend the night outside. As a child, I spent many nights sleeping outside in the grass, unable to enter the house.

But I don't let myself think about that. Old childhood memories of being forced to sleep in the backyard. The owls hooting. Trees waving in the night. The cold. Trying the handle on the front door, hoping maybe my father had changed his mind.

I am not a child anymore. I am not afraid. I *could* sleep in the forest. But the risk of getting lost is too great. If I wander too far and get turned around, I'll be eaten by the elements. It's cold, tonight.

The idea of calling for a car interests me for a moment, but then I remember: Sylian puts tracers in all employee phones. It's not something he bothers to check very often, except in special cases. And this— this would qualify as a special case.

I grab the phone from my pocket, give it a longing glance, and chuck it into the woods.

Goodbye, Sylian.

My walk down the road is slow and lonely. One car passes. When I see its headlights, I step back into the trees, careful not to be noticed. Other than that single, anonymous traveler, the road is abandoned. Quiet this late at night.

Hours pass. My feet start to tingle, numb from the effort. The wind cuts through my jacket. Walking *should* warm me up, but I'm only getting colder. The temperature must be dropping rapidly. A quick glance at the horizon tells me I'm heading in the right direction. The mountains are my landmark, keeping me heading West, toward a small town I visited often as a child.

Finally, I see it. Quaint lights in the distance. A clocktower. Pointed roofs. This is Baden-Baden, a spa town on the Western German border, butting up against the base of the Black Forest mountain range. It's famous for its hot springs, frequented by tourists who crave an idyllic, romantic getaway. "Baden" literally means "bath." Something I could use.

A cobblestone street opens up to greet me. It's the off season, so I won't find many tourists clogging up the atmosphere, consuming the village like ants on a corpse.

The first hotel I stumble across is a tiny inn. A wooden sign tells me its name is "*der Tressor,*" meaning "vault." The owners must be trying to convey a sense of safety. Of comfort.

It'll do, I think. The door squeaks as I enter the downstairs lobby. The waiting room is small, made entirely from wood paneling. Comfy chairs sit plush and still by a crackling fireplace.

Behind an enormous built-in desk, a sole proprietor stares at me. He looks alarmed. To this small man, I must look like a mystical thing. A timeless being emerging from the woods with no car, no reservation. It doesn't help that I haven't picked a popular arrival time.

"*Guten abend,*" he says, straightening his tie like he's been caught sleeping on the job. "Can I help you?" He switches to English. This is something that happens often. Even though I grew up in Germany, I'm often mistaken for an American. When I went to university in the states, I studied them closely. Observed their mannerisms and adopted them as my own.

"*Ich brauche ein Hotelzimmer,*" I tell him. "Right away."

"*Keine sorgen,*" he says, telling me not to worry.

I never do, I think. The man hurries to check me in, excepting cash or the first night. Thankfully, I always carry multiple currencies in my backpack, ready for any emergency. He passes me a solid metal key, and in no time at all, I'm making my way up the staircase to my new room.

It's a small accommodation at the end of the hall, but for what it lacks in size, it makes up for in charm. The bedding is a plush duvet complimented by striped pillows. Paisley wallpaper assault the walls. Most people would call it charming.

I hate it, I think.

Still, it's a roof. I fall into bed, pulling Zoe's poem out of my backpack and re-reading it once more.

Normally, on a difficult night like tonight, I'd mentally scan through my treasures. The ones in my suitcase. The ones Zoe stole. When I'm *really* struggling, I even open it up and take them out one by one, lining them up on the dresser to remind me of what I can achieve. To remind me that no one can hurt me and get away with it.

I try to conjure a mental image of these small items, but it doesn't come. It's not that I can't remember them, but more that I feel disconnected. Imagining my suitcase doesn't make me feel warm, tonight. It makes me feel sick.

The duvet envelopes me as I roll over and put a pillow over my head, trying to block out my own thoughts. I will myself to sleep, promising that the morning will be different.

I'm going to beat Zoe at her game. Get back to who I used to be. Emerge from this experience bigger and better, like I always do. I try to convince myself that victory is the goal. That victory is why I'm here. But something in me still cries out for attention. Something in me still wants to be heard.

It's a little voice that says maybe I don't *want* to win.

The voice collects evidence. Makes its case.

It's not like me to leave something as precious as my suitcase of treasures exposed and vulnerable. It's not like me to allow someone to get as close to me as Zoe has. It's not like me to be less than perfect. To make mistakes. To forget.

A terrible truth burns inside my chest, and I can't ignore it.

Maybe I'm tired of living this way. Tired of playing my own games. Of trying to control a world that doesn't want to be controlled. I've made myself the center of my own universe, and at first, it was an adrenaline rush. Caring about only my own needs and destroying anyone who didn't meet them made me feel powerful. But with every victory, with every vengeance, some small deposit was made within. A black, sticky tar inside my veins. A strange substance that distanced me from others. That made me less human. Sometimes, when I see kids playing in the park, I feel angry at them. Angry that they still have time to start over, and I don't. Angry that they can be so pure when I have suffered.

Maybe I left my suitcase unattended because I was tired of being angry. Maybe there's some alien piece of me within that wants to destroy its host.

Maybe I wanted to get caught.

18

ZOE

K *iel, Germany*

INGRID'S HOUSE IS A MAZE. Boxes are everywhere, cardboard edges stacked on top of each other, spiraling toward the ceiling. Miscellaneous items crowd the space, discarded into the void.

"Did you just move in?" I ask her, staring at the boxes.

Ingrid shakes her head. I lean in closer over one of the piles on the floor, and realize the items there aren't part of an ordinary household collection. These items are trash. Opened cans. Plastic bags. A cloth wrapper from an eaten piece of cheese.

The pile stirs. A mouse scampers out, annoyed at my presence.

"You have a guest," I tell her, motioning at the mouse.

"I have two," she says, leading me down a makeshift path carved between the mess. A plush carpet bends beneath my shoes, stained by spills and cigarette burns. Spiderwebs hang from the room's highest corner.

Ingrid is a hoarder.

She leads me into the living room, which is even more condensed than the entryway. Plastic tupperware bins line the back wall. A pile of clothes blocks another hallway. There's a TV sitting on a stand, with a small love seat in front of it. The loveseat is partially obscured by trash-bags tied at the top, but there's one cushion that's been left empty. An indentation in the cushion tells me this is where Ingrid sits.

Right on cue, she settles into the spot, picking up a pair of knitting needles. She's making something. A scarf, maybe. It's half finished. At her feet is a basket, clumps of yarn sitting within. They're tangled, as if she's used the yarn, undone her work, and reused it again.

"Where I should I sit?" I ask her.

She stares at me as if I've just asked the world's stupidest question.

"Anywhere you like," Ingrid answers, motioning around the room.

I try to calculate the safest place. There's nowhere appealing. I settle for leaning on the edge of the TV stand, pushing some things aside to make space for myself.

"Don't break anything." She watches as I shove a pile on the TV stand aside. "You'll owe me, if you break anything."

I glance down at what I've just pushed aside. It's a pile of newspapers. When I look back at Ingrid, I expect her to be smiling, but her expression tells me she's not joking.

"I'll be careful," I say. This seems to appease her, because she leans back in her seat, knitting needles clacking.

"I'm here to ask about your son," I begin.

"I don't know him anymore," she says, not looking at me. "I'm not sure I ever did."

"What was he like as a child?" I ask.

She sighs. "This is for the American University, yes?"

I nod. "Yes. The Columbia alumni history tree. We've picked one student from every year to feature." This is a lie I've told to gain access to information. Suddenly, I feel bad about it. But I need to know. Need to understand. And most importantly, need to confirm my suspicions.

"He was bright," she says. "Gifted. Johann was always good in school. Most especially with computers. He could speak to technology but not to other people. It was his gift."

She pauses, staring at me. "Are you going to make yourself useful or not?" She glances at the basket by my feet.

She wants me to untangle the yarn. I think about how many mice have run over the basket. Wonder about the strange smell in the house, and if whatever is causing it might be lying beneath the yarn. But I don't want to make her angry. I need her to relax. To be honest.

Despite the churning in my stomach, I pull the yarn out and find the end, untangling it a little at a time.

"Do you have any pictures of him?" I ask.

Ingrid sets down her needles and rises from the sofa, disappearing into the mess. She's gone so long I start to worry she might never return, but then she appears again, carrying a cardboard box. She plops it down in front of me, grunting with the weight of it.

"Have a look," she says, picking up her knitting again.

I use the edge of my shoe to lift the corner of the box. There's piles of photographs within, disorganized and unprotected. Old polaroids sit scattered among printed 4 x 6s and 8 x 10s. The photos are warped in some places, telling me they've been exposed to water. Colors run on their edges. The polaroids are faded and aging.

Carefully, I reach into the box and pull out a picture of a young boy, wearing a tie and corduroy pants.

"This is him?" I ask.

She nods.

In the photograph, there's a man standing next to him. He's tall and imposing, a dark beard covering his face. There's a coldness in his eyes as he looks down at the boy in his photograph, like he's trying to mentally reassemble him. Trying to make him into something pleasing.

"Is this his father?"

I turn the photo around and Ingrid looks lost for a second, like she's been dropped into her current body from some far away place.

"Yes," she says. That's him.

"Did they get along?"

Ingrid sniffs. "How American."

"What do you mean?"

"Always worrying about what's ideal. Not what's practical." I sit still, showing no offense. "No," she says. "They didn't 'get along.' Armand wanted great things for his children. He was American, in fact, like you."

"He was?"

"Yes," she says. "He owned a company that brought him here for a work-related trip. We met when I was hired as a translator. Our first child was an accident, and when I got pregnant, he married me out of necessity. He could not stay in Germany without the visa, and wanted to be around his children to make sure they would thrive. As you can see," she motions around the room. "I'm hardly a homemaker."

"What kind of parent was he?"

"Simple," she shrugs. "He rewarded achievement, and punished mediocrity. He believed in their greatness."

"*Their* greatness?"

"Of course," Ingrid continues. "Armand was nothing if not an equal opportunity employer. He held Mia and Johanne to the same standards. Mia met them, more often than not. But Johann... the boy struggled."

"You talk about him like he's not your son." The words slip out of my mouth before I have time to decide if I should say them or not. I worry I've offended her, but Ingrid doesn't blink. She just keeps knitting, the needles flying back in forth, clacking like a metronome. The sound is rhythmic and disturbing.

"I always liked to keep distance from my children." She says it without making eye contact. "Armand pointed out my affliction might be passed onto them. He was right, of course. He was better suited to parent than I was. We lived together, of course, given the time. It wasn't appropriate back then, for a mother to separate from her family. But I stayed in the guest house with my treasures. I would visit the children in the main house for dinner, then retreat, leaving them be. They were better off with Armand."

I dig through the box again, pulling out another picture of the boy. This time, he's standing outside a playground. There's a girl next to him. She's taller, and looks a couple years older, but has the same coloring. Those same eyes.

"Is this her?" I hold up the picture.

"Don't," Ingrid says. "Put it away."

I listen to her instructions and tuck the photo back in the box.

"What was she like?" I ask.

"Brilliant," Ingrid says. "According to Armand, anyway. She

had his wits. His mind. His cleverness. She rose to every challenge. But that wasn't why I loved her." Ingrid's voice becomes a whisper, soft and lost. "I loved Mia because she would bring me leaves from the garden. Leaves in different colors each season. She pressed them between the pages of her books so they would dry out, then make them into bookmarks. She left them outside the guest house door. Every week, another leaf."

"She was Armand's favorite," I say.

Ingrid nods. "I wish she hadn't been."

"What do you mean?"

"If she had only been less bright, a little slower, Armand would not have trained her in her studies so. He taught her Latin. French. Algebra. But it came at a cost."

"Was he unkind to them?"

Ingrid nods. "He would give them tests on what they learned. Make them compete against each other. The child who lost would spend the night outside."

"That's abuse," I say.

She waves a hand as if she's swatting the words away. "He wanted them to be great!"

"Greatness isn't enough to make a person a person," my voice rises.

"What do you mean by that?" She asks.

"Children need balance. Greatness should come as a byproduct of what we love. It should come from wanting to make the world better, or make something that helps others. Teaching children to strive for greatness alone builds a shell of a person. A computer can be great. A robot can be great. People need more."

"I suppose you think I didn't give them what they needed?" The question is a challenge. An invitation to shame her.

"When they were sleeping outside, did you let them in the guest house?" I ask.

She stares at me. Notices I'm not done with the basket yet.

"Are you going to continue or shall I show you out?" Her voice is crisp and cold. It sends a shiver down my spine. I pretend to continue untangling the yarn.

"Johann couldn't keep up with the work his father assigned. He was the one who fell behind. But when Mia disappeared, Johann was all Armand had left. It became a blessing and a curse. All Johann ever wanted was to be Armand's pride and joy, and when he became it by default, it still did not satisfy him."

"He never felt enough," I summarize.

Ingrid nods.

"How did Mia disappear?" I ask the question even though I already know the answer.

For a moment, Ingrid looks like she wants to answer me, but instead, she holds up the scarf she's knitting.

"It's blue, isn't it?"

"Yes," I tell her.

"It reminds me of the ocean."

"Me too," I say.

"It won't do." Suddenly, she untangles her work, pulling it apart. She slams the yarn back into the basket.

"What about red?" I ask, removing red yarn from within.

"Too much like blood," She says.

"The purple?" I hold up a tangled purple mess.

"Mia's favorite color," Ingrid answers, running her fingers over the yarn. She closes her hand around the edge. "Do you know Johann now?"

"I think I do," I tell her.

"What is he like?" She pauses, searching. "Is he like his father, or is he like me?"

"Neither," I say. "He's become something else."

"I didn't want to give it to him. My affliction. Didn't want him to collect, like I do."

I don't have the heart to tell her that Logan *is* a collector, but in a way more terrible than anything she can imagine.

"Do you think it's true that a child is destined to become one thing or another?"

"I don't know," I tell her. "I was left by my Dad. My husband's family wasn't good to him. But I can honestly tell you we're not like Johann. We make choices, every day. Choices that show us who we are. And we're not like him."

She rises from her seat. "I'd like you to leave, now," She tells me.

I stand, honoring her wishes. My feet kick boxes aside as I make my way back toward the front door. I'm almost to the entryway when I stop. There's one more thing I have to say.

"He was wrong."

"Who?" She asks, her voice faraway.

"Armand. He wasn't the better parent. You could have been a better parent than him, if you'd trusted yourself enough to try."

She takes this in for a moment. Opens her mouth like a fish underwater. No sound comes out. She picks up more yarn from the basket, wrapping it around her needle.

"I'll start over," she says to no one in particular. "I'll do better this time."

"If you want to do better," I tell her. "Give me what I need." I wander back toward the living room and open up the box again, pulling out a pile of yellowed paperwork. "I could have taken them, but I didn't want to do it without your blessing."

"Those are Mia's," she says, her voice pained.

"Yes," I agree.

"What do you need them for?"

"For Johann," I tell her. "For his soul."

She thinks about it. Then nods. "Take them," she says. With her blessing, I do. They're frail and thin, fraying over many years, but they're what I need.

Once the papers are in my hand, I leave as fast as I can, trying not to give Ingrid the chance to change her mind.

Later, I charter a boat to take me to an island off the coast of Kiel. It's the place where I've left a puzzle for Logan. A puzzle that was missing a piece, until now.

19

LOGAN

B *aden-Baden, Germany.*

IT TAKES me half a day to get to Kiel. I hate to admit it, but working for Sylian has made me soft. I've gotten used to the ease with which I travelled. The ability to call for a car and have it arrive right on time, ready to take me where I wish. Now, I have to rely on the same transport available to the rest of the world.

My first stop in the morning is the bank. There's a small establishment here in Baden-Baden that will allow me to withdrawal funds. My accounts tied to Sylian are closed. No surprise there. But my private accounts remain untouched. The biggest of these is an offshore account in a blind Swiss account. It's exactly as I left it. Full, and bursting.

I'm going to be just fine, I tell myself.

I take out a few grand in cash and make my way the nearest *System & Komponenten*— a German computer store.

I have to leave town to find one, so I check out of the hotel and take my bags with me before setting off in a rental car.

When I reach the store, I buy a computer in cash, borrowing their Wi-Fi to log on to my own private VPN.

Sylian isn't the only one who can set up a secured network.

Once I'm on, I access my private files, stored remotely in a cloud that only I can access. There's a folder dedicated to fake identities. One I've kept separate from Sylian just in case I ever needed to disappear.

I select a new name, social security number, and credit card, and use the information to set up a cell phone. Anonymity isn't always the best way to hide. Actions taken by a ghost with no thumbprint register as more suspicious than those taken by someone identifiable. That's why using someone else's image is an excellent way to keep your activities private. When Interpol tracks the disruption, the trail will lead them to someone else's doorstep.

I have one more purchase to make before I leave Baden-Baden. A cell phone. My new identity allows me to purchase it without a hitch.

It's only when I'm fully armed with a computer and phone that I start to feel like myself again. If I am a warrior, these are my weapons. Sylian doesn't define me. Sylian was lucky to *have* me.

Still, the drive to Kiel gives me too much time to think about what's happened. A curving road cuts through meadows and grass. The emptiness makes me wonder who I would be if I were dropped in the middle of nowhere with no resources. No secret accounts. No hidden valuables. If someone left me to start from zero with nothing to my name, would I make it?

Yes, I think to myself. *You would make it because you are strong.*

I think about Gabrielle. Remember the satellite images I've collected over the years since we parted. Fuzzy pictures of Gabrielle at her window, in nothing but a robe, looking out across the glass like she can feel me watching her.

I wonder if she felt like I do now? The thought surprises me. I've never paused to consider how Gabrielle felt when she lost her dream job at C.E.R.N. Some would argue she lost it *because* of me, but in truth, she lost it because of her own choices. Because she wasn't good enough to operate without me. If she had only accepted my help— been brave enough to let me into her life to guide her— I wouldn't have had to sabotage her work. She didn't *have* to let the experience crush her. She could have risen from it better. Stronger. As a mentor, I was disappointed she didn't get up again. I wish she had. It would have presented me with a challenge, at least. A game to play. I would have followed her from job to job, creating trouble for her anywhere she went, maybe even ending her life eventually. But I never got the chance, because she didn't get back up to fight again. She hid. Hid behind those curtains. She wasn't worthy. Wasn't interesting anymore.

It's ironic. I cost her a job. And now she's taken mine. This must be Zoe's strategy. An eye for an eye. A tooth for a tooth.

I am not like Gabrielle, I smile to myself. *I will not crumble. Yes, this stings. But I will deal with Sylian in my own time. I will not hide behind the curtains.*

The drive to Kiel is long, and bright. The sun hurts my eyes the entire way there. There were many things I never liked about my hometown, and the warmth of the sun during summertime was one of them. As a child, I always felt it was mocking me by choosing to be cheerful in the midst of my despair.

When I reach the city, my stomach turns. Pastel buildings reach for the sky. A beautiful bridge curves over the horizon in an arc. The smell of saltwater makes my nose burn.

There's a tug within. I didn't expect to have this reaction. I can't name the feeling. It's somewhere between wanting to flee, and desperate longing. Like I wish I could stay in my hometown forever, but run away at the same time. My car rolls past a park, where children play on a *Klettergerüst*. A jungle gym. Their laughter makes my ears burn. Reminds me of a time long ago, when I watched my sister swing from the bars.

"*Gute arbeit, Mia!*" My father cried. "Excellent, how strong you are."

I remember the way he looked at me when I tried to follow her. When I fell from the bars— unable to cross like she did— he left me there. Sitting in the dirt. Crying like the weak child I was. We found out a week later the fall had fractured my collarbone.

I was never as good as Mia in his eyes. Never as strong. Never as fast. Never as smart. She was like *him* in so many ways. I used to wonder if all of his talents had been passed onto her in some freak genetic accident, leaving Mia with all his brilliance, and me with nothing but my mother's eccentricities.

"Stop collecting!" My father would shout at me when he stumbled onto my hiding places, finding yo-yos and chip bags, old soda cans and earthworms. "You will end up like your mother."

An image of my suitcase flashes before my eyes. It's filled with the only trinkets I *allow* myself to collect as an adult. I'm willing to go to such great lengths to get it back. Maybe I *am* like her.

No, I think to myself. *That's where Father was wrong.*

Mia may have inherited Father's brilliance. His intelligence. The ease with which he navigated the world. She even got his height. But she got Mother's heart. She got mother's gentleness. Her softer side.

Father's heart— his wicked nature, his willingness to achieve what he wanted by any means possible— *that* was passed onto me. And by passing that onto me, he enabled me to eliminate my competition. To come out ahead as the victor, eventually.

I'd hoped that by demonstrating my commitment to winning, father would love me more than Mia. Of course, that's not what happened. He missed her so that he drank himself to death not long after. Now, he's lying next to her in the Earth in Kiel's only cemetery. Still, I like to think if he were alive, he'd have come around by now. That if he could see all I've done, he'd be proud. That he'd finally acknowledge the way in which we're similar. That he'd see me as his protege.

"Look at me now, Vater," I smile to myself as I pull into a parking lot by the harbor. I read Zoe's poem one more time, stopping at the relevant stanza.

"Another clue awaits you
In the place from whence you came
Keep your head on, even **keil**
"Captain" means its name."

My lungs expand, breathing in the terrible salt air as I exit the rental car. I've always hated the ocean. It's too unpredictable. Unable to be controlled.

A quick walk down the harbor helps me find what I'm looking for. There, among the moored sailboats and tiny fishing vessels, is the boat I'm looking for.

She's named it "Der Kapitänin," the German word for

Captain. She's chosen the feminine form over the masculine form, which would read "Kapitän." It's her little joke, I'm sure. Her way of trying to tell me who's *really* in charge.

A few moments later and I'm heading toward the open water, settling into my seat once I've charted the correct course. I open Zoe's letter again.

"The spot is where you left her
The place is where she died
You took her pride and left her there
We wonder if you cried?"

She's sending back to the island where it happened. The place where I left her.

The rock where Mia died.

Later, I call Mike. I tell him I'm coming home.

"I want you in my arms," he says. "Don't get lost."

But I already am lost, I think.

It's almost midnight, and I can't sleep. I'm in my cozy hotel bed. The pillows are plush. The duvet is the perfect weight. But sleep won't come.

On impulse, I jump out of bed and slip on my jeans. The hotel is so quiet I feel the need to tiptoe to the elevator, as if I'm a teenager sneaking out past curfew. The elevator takes me down to the lobby, and I practically run to the double doors. The cool night air is light on my shoulders.

I need to walk. Need to think. Need to find answers and quiet my mind.

Can I do what needs to be done?

The bars are still open. Rowdy drunks pour out onto the sidewalk, glasses overflowing. I don't know where I'm going, but I keep walking anyway, sensing that I'll know when to stop. When I see what I need, I'll know.

Across the street, a building towers over me. Spiraled turrets reach for the sky. Stained glass windows reflect the city lights.

It's a church.

It's difficult to say what affiliation the church belongs to. The name is spelled out in German, which I don't speak. Maybe it's the name of a Saint, or of letters. It's all just gibberish to me.

I approach the building's entrance, pushing on the heavy wooden doors. They creak open. I'm surprised the church is accessible so late. Then again, something about that feels right. Like churches *should* stay open all the time.

I settle into one of the wooden pews. There's no one else around except a woman a few aisles behind me, leaning against the pew, praying.

The scent of polished wood burns my nose as I inhale. Light floods in from the stained glass windows. A watery image of Logan's face swims in my mind as I think about what I will do. What I *must* do.

Suddenly, there's a tap on my shoulder. It's the woman. She has kind eyes, and she's holding a rosary. She's older. The wrinkles by her eyes remind me of a painting, like someone has put them there on purpose.

"*Geht es dir gut*?" She asks.

"I'm sorry, I don't speak—" I start to say.

"English, then," She answers me in near perfect English. "Do you need anything?"

"Do you work here?"

She shakes her head. "I'm a patron. I prefer to pray late." She motions around the chapel. "It's quiet, you see."

"Yes, I do," I nod.

"I see all kinds of people come in this late at night," she sits down next to me. "Sometimes they're looking for a place to sleep. Sometimes they need somebody to talk to." She pauses, staring at the tall ceilings. "Is there something on your mind?"

"There's a man," I tell her. "He's made my life— difficult."

"He's not your husband, is he?"

I laugh. "No. This person hunts me. He stalks me."

"I see," she nods, serious. "He takes your sense of safety."

"Yes," I tell her. "And I hated him for a long time. But the more I learn about him, the more I see what we have in common."

"Like?" She asks.

"His Father was never interested in him. He's competitive, like me. Aloof, like me. We've been through similar childhood experiences. It makes it hard, to do what I need to do."

Her eyes widen. She looks like she wants to ask me more, but stops herself.

"I'm the only one who can beat him at his own game," I tell her.

"The police?" She asks, hopeful.

"They can't," I shake my head. "They've had dozens of opportunities to catch him, and they haven't. He's a ghost. I'm the only one who can meet him on his level. Who can bait him into a trap. I'm the only one who can stop him. I know it, deep down in my bones. And if I don't stop him, he'll hurt other people. People who don't deserve it. But to stop him, I may have to do something... wrong. "

"I could find a priest," she says, suddenly looking around the chapel. "A priest for you to talk to."

"No," I say, suddenly certain. "I want to know what *you* think."

"What *I* think?"

"Yes," I take a breath. "If this man and I are similar in so many ways— if I *see* myself in him— how can I fault him for being the animal he is?"

She chews on this, looking at the rafters again.

"I cook, you know," she says without looking at me. "I make all kinds of things. My daughter likes some better than others." She laughs. "But what I've found is you can take the same ingredients, and make a different dish." She leans in, puts her hand on my knee. "It's not what you experience in life, but what you do with it that makes you who you are."

I don't realize I'm crying until I feel a tear drop fall on my hand. "What about forgiveness?" I say.

"There is forgiveness for all, of this I'm certain," she answers. "But only he can ask for it. There is redemption for all who seek it. One is never too far gone to try and find a light back."

"Like, a choice?" I say.

She nods.

"He gave me a choice once," I tell her.

"Mmm," she answers, not asking more.

A choice, I think. The lights pour in those windows again, and suddenly everything clicks into place. I know what I have to do. I need to make a change to my final puzzle. Not just for Logan's soul, but for mine.

The woman leaps in surprise as I pull her into a hug.

"Thank you," I say.

"*Gerne geschen,*" she answers.

21

LOGAN

E*insam Island, the Baltic Sea.*

ROCKS CLATTER as my small boat reaches the shore. It's been a peaceful journey, but a long one. A trip to Einsam island from Keil takes six hours in decent winds. Now, the sun is setting, and angry clouds are gathering on the horizon.

"*Einsam*" means "solitude" in German. The island is aptly named. This small archipelago isn't technically even large enough to constitute a full island. It's more like a rock in the middle of the ocean, independent from other atolls. From a distance, it looks like a giant turtle emerging from the sea, its back a rounded shell.

Tourists don't come here, mainly because there's nothing interesting to see. No one lives on Einsam. There are no businesses, or shops. Einsam was once used for biological research. Scientists would make camp, here, to better observe and measure the water levels, making the case for climate change by monitoring rising tides caused by melting ice caps. But now, that argument needs no further evidence. Their research outposts have long been closed, leaving nothing behind but abandoned shacks and rusting equipment.

Children who grow up in Keil know about Einsam only because we were forbidden from visiting. From a young age, our parents warned us not to take our sailboats out so far. Yes, almost every family in Kiel owns a boat, and children grow up learning to sail just as they learn to walk. But Einsam was always forbidden. At night, the tides come in high, smashing against the rocks in a violet, angry surge. It makes leaving not only difficult, but dangerous. Decades before I was born, two teenagers went missing and were later found on. It was a local tragedy. The stuff of urban legend. Ever since, the place was deemed "dangerous." Neighborhood coalitions worked on getting the word out to concerned parents, and for many years, no one else was stranded on the island again.

No one, until Mia.

My shoes crunch over the rocks. Cold, bitter water soaks my feet. It doesn't bother me. The feeling is familiar. Last time I was here, I came into my own. The last time I was here, I stepped into my destiny.

To trick Mia into coming to Einsam, I used her weaknesses against her. Told her that I knew a girl from her science class, Ellana, was planning to use a secret on Einsam to her benefit. Mia was always in competition with Ellana. It took Mia great effort to outscore Ellana on every exam. And now, the school science fair was fast approaching. The science fair was Mia's best opportunity to make Father proud. And there was nothing Mia loved doing more than making Father proud.

"Ellana said she found something out there that would

help her with her experiment," I lied. "Objects left over from the climate change researchers." Mia's eyebrows raised in that curious way she had. Mia's project involved greenhouse gases. She was hooked.

It's not hard to guess where I'm supposed to go on the island. I knew it as soon as I read Zoe's poem.

The spot is where you left her
The place is where she died
You took her pride and left her there
We wonder if you cried?

Mia's body was found in one of the old buildings used by researchers on the island. An expansive, metal warehouse that was once used by oil companies to store excess chemicals. When the researchers came, they repurposed it for the good of the planet in an act of cosmic justice. It's an echo of my own adventure, here. I've been brought to the island by Zoe— a woman I once stranded on an island. It was my time with Mia that inspired the plan. We've come full circle.

And I'll come out on top again, I think as I make my way toward the metal warehouse. It sits beside a rock formation, holes in its roof. There's no windows on the warehouse, and only a single door that serves as both the entrance and exit. This was a place built for utility, not for comfort.

The door screeches as I pull it open. It takes substantial effort on my part. The metal is twisted, rusting over all these years.

Inside the building, dust hangs in the air. A powdery, dry scent coats my lungs. The light from the door allows me to see what's directly in front of me, but little else. A plastic bucket. An abandoned toolbox. The sad remains of the past. My stomach flips, surprising me. Somehow, I'd been expecting to find Mia's body, even though I know they recovered it and brought it back to shore.

My fingers carve a path along the wall, seeking a light switch. I'm not sure if there's still electrical service to the island, but I notice a solar panel on the roof. The scientists studying climate change must have insisted on installing an eco-friendly option.

My hand finds the switch. I flip it, and the place comes to life with light. Recessed flashbulbs turn on above me. There's a snapping sound over my shoulder, and I whirl around to discover the door has snapped itself shut. A quick check of the handle reveals that it's locked. There's a mechanism attached to the hinges— a spring and pulley. Zooey must have connected it to the light switch.

She thinks she's trapped me, I smile. The idea is ridiculous. When I'm ready to leave, I'll find my way out. I'm untrappable. Still, her effort is a cute attempt.

A scan of the room proves that it's relatively empty. Tile floors. Beige walls. Cobwebs strung from the rafters. It's a windowless box with no character and nothing to offer, except for a display set up against the far wall.

My footsteps send echoes cascading across the room as I approach the display. It's been crafted from items found within the space. A metal desk with locking drawers. A plastic bucket serves as a replacement for a missing leg, propping the desk up. Lights that match the ones overhead, rewired to illuminate the display, bringing attention specifically to this section of the room.

In the center of the desk— in a place of prominence— sits an old ham radio. I put on the headphones and flip the switch. No static. It's not operational. The back panel practically falls off when I move to examine it, revealing a mess of wires within. Someone has played with the radio's insides, either attempting to repair or destroy it. I'm not sure which. Some of the cables within are brighter in color, making me think they've been added in recent years. They stand out against the faded plastic coating of the older, surrounding wires.

Above the desk is a shelf, on which stands little vials, lined up in a row. They look like something used by the researchers to collect samples, except each one has been marked with an unusual label. "*Blood,*" reads one. "*Dust,*" reads another. There's three vials in total. In front of each sits an envelope.

Suddenly, the radio comes to life. A sound emanates from the headphones. I grab them and shove them over my ears so I don't miss the message.

"Logan." It's Zoe's voice. I recognize it immediately. The sound sends a strange, electric current rippling down my arms. "Pick one substance that shows you can change. Otherwise, meet acid rain."

As soon as it's over, the message plays again. And again. It's on a loop. The lack of additional information is frustrating. I want to ask Zoe questions. Want to make her suffer. Instead, I'm faced with a proxy version of her. A version I can't touch. Can't destroy.

"*Pick one substance that shows you can change. Otherwise, meet acid rain.*"

My eyes scan the ceiling, wondering if Zoe means literal acid rain. There's a set of fire sprinklers rigged to the rafters. They look original, but maybe she's connected to them to vials of acid. It would be a bold move. One that allows another to suffer. It would be uncharacteristic of Zoe, to torture another person, even her worst enemy. I'm tempted to throw the contest. To get it wrong on purpose just to call her bluff. But the stakes are high if I'm wrong. Too high.

My attention switches to the vials in front of me. The label on the first reads "*Blood.*" I notice a silver knife in front of it. The label on the second reads "*Dust.*" There's a hammer and a rock in front of it. On the third, the label reads "*Tears.*" In front of it sits an envelope. It's labeled, simply, "From Mia."

It's clear I'm supposed to choose a substance to place in one of the vials, and then deposit it somewhere. But where? I re-read Zoe's poem.

> *"Pick one vial*
> > *Not one more*
> > *Don't you trust*
> > *That fickle floor."*

A quick scan of the floor reveals flat, decaying tiles, featuring the same speckled pattern. At first, all the tiles look similar, until I notice one that stands out from all the others. The pattern is swirling yes, but it isn't made of dots. My knees crack as I bend down closer to the tile, trying to make out what's there. Words scroll in a line, cursive handwriting spelling out a command.

"*Repent, repent, repent.*" The word has been written a thousand times, following the same loop the dots on the original tile once made. They're meant to be a command. An instruction.

She wants me to feel sorry for what I've done, I think to myself. The idea shows how little Zoe understands about the world. She focuses on internal life. The things you can't see— they are the things that mean the most to her. She could ask me to give up money. To give up power. But instead she wants me to feel— *sorry?* An emotion of no benefit to her. Maybe she believes if I regret my actions, I'll let her live once I win our little game.

Keep dreaming, I think, bending closer to the tile. In the center sits a small hole surrounded by gold metal. It looks like a drain of some kind. This must be where I'm meant to deposit the given substance I choose.

I return to the vials, plotting my course. Out of interest, I pick up the knife in front of blood to examine it. There's a crackling from the radio, and a back panel opens. A tiny digital screen rises from within, displaying a clock. It's set to ten minutes. There's a beeping sound, and the countdown begins. A small pressure sensor sits where the knife was previously positioned. Touching the weapon activated the clock. They must all be rigged that way.

I bet there's no acid rain at all, I laugh to myself. Zoe doesn't have the courage for it. Doesn't have the teeth. Still, I play along, delighted she's trying to walk on the wild side.

I turn the knife over in my hand, thinking about how easy it would be to cut myself and drop my blood into the vial. But then... would Zoe be so crude? I'm not sure. Mostly likely, no. Still, I drop the knife into my pocket. It's a beautiful weapon. One I'd like the chance to use on Zoe, one day, in a beautiful act of irony.

I move onto the next option, which is dust. The small rock that sits in front of the vial is a delicate one that reminds me of shale. There's a hammer beside it. It would be easy to crush into a fine powder. I immediately eliminate it as a choice. Zoe likes things to have meaning. The rock means nothing, except perhaps that it reminds her of the landscape in Yosemite, where we first went encountered one another without pretense or false identities.

The final vial is labeled *"Tears."* There, in front of it, sits an envelope with the single word "Mia," scrawled across its surface. The word "tears" sets off a trigger in my mind. I take another look at Zoe's poem:

"The spot is where you left her
　　The place is where she died
　　You took her pride and left her there
　　We wonder if you cried?"

Of all the choices, this is the one that aligns with Zoe's theme.

Repent.

I want nothing to do with this envelope. No piece of me cares what's inside. But it's part of Zoe's game, and I can't win without all the information. Reluctantly, I open it, ripping the top of the envelope off with care to avoid damaging what's inside.

I turn the envelope upside down, and yellowed, crumpled pages fall on the desk. The pages display hurried paragraphs in German. The handwriting is impossible to ignore, because I grew up comparing it to my own. Where my letters slanted to the left in a chaotic dance, my sister's cursive was always organized. Perfect. Just like her.

These words were written by Mia. An insignia on the top reads *"International Fellowship for Scientific Advancement,"* or *"I.F.S.A."* The papers she used were left over from the scientists who once did their research, here, which means Mia could only have found them on the island. She wrote these letters while trapped in this compound. While trapped here because of me.

There's only one person Zoe could've gotten these letters from. *She's been to see Mother.* The thought makes my heart pound. I've never read these letters. I heard, of course, that Mia had left some writing behind upon her death. But Father never let me see what she said. I assumed it was because she outed me in her final message. Father wouldn't have believed it of course. Wouldn't think me capable of besting his favorite child.

The timer on the clock dings, snapping me back to the present moment. The display tells me I have six minutes left. There's no time to reminisce. Without further hesitation, I settle in, and begin to read.

"I'M RELIEVED to have found this place. Johann took the boat, but I know he will come back. He would not leave me if there were not an emergency. Maybe the tide rose and washed it off the shore, and he swam to get it. He will come back when he finds it. I just have to stay well until then."

"IN A NIGHT AND A DAY, Johann has not returned. I am worried something has happened to him. What if he has drowned in the sea? He will come back. He will be alright. He must be alright."

"THREE DAYS and no sign of Johann. I have attempted to rewire the radio to call for help to save us both, if he is still out there. Maybe he is fighting as I am, to stay alive. There is no fresh water here. No food. The sun is strong. I've attempted to light a signal fire, hoping a passing boat might see it. I've foraged for fruit in the surrounding trees, but do not know what is safe to eat. I eat it anyway, as I am so hungry. And the thirst. There is water everywhere around me, but none to drink. None to drink."

"MOTHER. *Father. Johann. I tried. I am still trying.*

The flowers, here, are purple. My favorite color, even still. Even now.

Love. Forever, sorry.

- M."

THE WORDS SWIM on the page. Mia's writing becomes indecipherable, swirling into shapes I've never seen before.

She didn't believe I left her here on purpose.

How could she not see it? How could she believe in me, even after I abandoned her here? Tricked her into going to see the research outpost, sneaking away with the boat at the first opportunity. When I got back to the mainland, I told my parents I didn't know where Mia was, even though I knew exactly where they'd find her. I could have saved her at any point over the course of week, but chose time and time again to keep the secret to myself. My parents knew the truth, of course, once they read these letters. Now that I've read them as well, I understand what came to follow. Forced therapy appointments with psychologists who never understood me. The police must have assumed I left her on accident. Must have told my parents I was traumatized from an unknown experience. "Maybe she fell overboard," they must have justified. "He is just a boy. Perhaps he was afraid." They would have found a thousand explanations to avoid looking the truth in the eye.

But my parents. They always knew. Deep down, they knew the truth about me. Everything changed after Mia's body was found. There was a coldness between us. My Father despised me even more than usual. My Mother went through the motions of parenting, but wanted nothing to do with me. After reading these letters, I know why.

Mia never gave up on me, I think. *Even after I left her.*

Gears turn in my brain. There's a tightness in my throat. Once again, I find myself jealous of my sister, even when she's no longer living. Even when she's no longer someone I can compete against. How is it that she's capable of feeling things I'm not? Where does this deep, unshakeable belief in good come from? How did she find it, when the world is so cold? How could she love me, when I am what I am?

Whatever trait she inherited, it's one I don't have. It's the same one that lives within Zoe. The same one I've tried to squash, because I know I can never exhibit it myself. It takes a certain kind of courage, to be good when faced with evil. I think about the children I saw, laughing on the playground, filled with hope, and possibility. How I'll never be like them again.

There's a burning in my eyes, and suddenly I'm crying. Not for Mia. I can't cry for her pain, for her experience, although I'd like to. It's just not something I'm capable of. I cry for myself. Cry for the things I'll never be. The feelings I'll never know. I wish I were different. I *want* to be different. There was a time when I though I could try. Maybe I'd never feel emotions the same way as others, but I thought perhaps I could still live as one of them, creating my own unique code of behavior to fit in. To be a part of something. But now, it's too late for me. I will never be a person worth believing in. Will never be a person like Mia.

Tears. I grab the vial and collect a few drops off my face. They form a pool at the bottom of the small container. A glance at the timer tells me I have one minute left. I make my way to the tile, leaning over the metal circle in the center. With care, I tip the vial over, letting the tears spill into the hole in the center. There's a moment, then: the clock beeps. The countdown freezes.

A popping sound echoes near my feet. The tile opens, revealing a hollow space underneath. There's another envelope inside. Another clue. I take it, glad to be one step closer to retrieving my suitcase and the valuables within.

My footsteps ring out across the space as I make my way to the door. It opens with ease, fully unlocked now. The sunlight strikes my eyes face when I step outside, its warmth making me shy away.

I'm about to walk to the boat— to launch myself away from this forbidden place— but I stop in my tracks. There's something I need to do. Something I *have* to know.

Sand gets in my shoes as I run back to the building I just exited. There's a sheet of plastic in a pile of junk outside. It's an expansive, waterproof tarp once used by researchers to cover their equipment in bad weather. I grab it, carrying back inside with me.

The metal blade that was positioned next to the "*Blood*" vial is still in my pocket. I head back toward the tile and snap it shut, putting it back in the proper spot. My arms stretch as I balance the tarp overhead, using one hand to keep it in place. With the other hand, I position the blunt handle of the knife between my teeth. In a sweeping motion, I cut my palm against the sharp, shiny blade.

Drops of my blood drip onto the tile, spilling onto that golden circle in the center. I wait a moment, wondering if Zoe really has it in her to follow through with her promise of acid rain.

Then, there's a hissing noise. The fire sprinklers open wide, spraying liquid across the room. Sizzling sounds flood the space. All around me, the dotted, patterned tiles erode.

Holes appear between the tiles, first as tiny pinpricks, growing wider as the acid strikes new areas.

I let one hand emerge from beneath my tarp, allowing a few drops of acid to coat the back of my palm. My skin burns. Involuntarily, my hand shakes beneath the damage. I let myself feel the pain. Try to enjoy the change in my exterior, now permanently marred. It's evidence of a conquest. Evidence of a challenge I met.

Keeping the tarp overhead, I make my way back to the door, hurrying when I notice my shoes are melting. I step outside to safety, looking inward at the melting, twisting heap within. Support beams twist. The metal desk hangs too low on one side. It reminds me of a Salvador Dalí painting. If the sprinklers continue, the building will collapse, destroying the past in a burning, sticky end.

I know one thing for sure, now. *Zoe is willing to torture. Willing to kill.*

Maybe I *have* made some impact. Maybe, despite her resistance, I'm winning the battle after all. Zoe is becoming more like me, *because* of me. It's an unavoidable, unwinnable game. She can't win. But even if I *do* lose and she beats me, she'll have lost anyway, because I'll continue to exist in some form, having turned her into someone very much like me.

When I get back to the boat and let the sails open wide, the thought makes me smile all the way back to shore.

Zoe has created a game she can't win.

22

ZOE

S*anta Monica, California.*

WHEN MY PLANE lands at LAX, Mike is there, waiting for me. He's standing in the parking lot, leaning on the exterior door of a beat up old van with fake license plates. The car comes compliments of Cassandra, who thought Mike could continue using it for his furniture business when all is said is done. Later, when I tell him why she made sure he got a van, he rolls his eyes. "I'll sell it," he tells me. He hates when Cassandra inserts herself into his business, evenly subtly.

When I run to the parking lot, Mike scoops me into his arms. He holds me for what feels like forever, running his hands through my hair. He smells familiar. I realize that— for the first time in weeks— I feel safe. As if everything is going to be okay, now that we're together.

A quick trip up the 405 brings us to Santa Monica. The smell of the beach hangs in the air. "The safe house is *here?*" I ask Mike. "That's convenient."

He shakes his head. "Zoe, these guys have safe houses everywhere. Every city in the world. The stories Smith has told me—"

"I don't want to know."

"You wouldn't believe what they do!"

"Still don't want to know," I tell him, pretending to cover my ears. "When all this done, we're going to live peacefully as a carpenter and a woman in hospitality. We're going to have normal, tragic lives where nothing interesting happens."

"God, that sounds so good," Mike sighs.

The van purrs as we pull into an underground parking lot beneath a dated apartment building on Santa Monica boulevard. When we reach the elevator, Mike doesn't push any buttons.

"Well?" I ask him.

"I'm pausing for effect," he smiles at me. "Are you ready?"

"Yes."

"It's so cool, Zoe. This is James Bond shit."

"I get it," I tell him.

"You're watching right?"

"Only getting older by the minute," I say.

Mike reaches for the elevator buttons, but instead of selecting a single floor, he holds down the buttons for two floors at the same time. Floor eight, and floor three. The elevator leaps into action, heading not up, but down.

"That's it?" I ask.

"What do you *mean* that's it?!" Mike rubs his temples. "It's a secret code to make the elevator go *down*. As in, to a floor no one knows about."

"Makes sense," I nod.

"I can't believe you're not wowed by this!" Mike says,

frustrated. "Do you need to see it again?" He reaches toward the panel of buttons, ready to take us back upstairs.

"I got it," I say, grabbing his hand in mid-air.

The elevator doors open, spilling us into the living room of a windowless apartment. Despite the fact it's underground, efforts have been made to create a warm environment. False curtains hang on the wall, giving the effect of openness even though there's no windows behind them. On the far wall, a painted mural displays trees and animals. There's a large couch in the center of the room, in front of the TV. On a nearby recliner sits a man with sandy blonde hair and enormous muscles.

"Mike?" I ask, suddenly concerned. "Who is this?"

"This is Smith," Mike says, nodding at the man on the couch. "He's on our side."

"Nobody's on our side except us," I say.

Smith stands, reaching out to shake my hand. "Admire what you're doing. I always hated that guy."

"Thanks," I tell him.

"Sylian wanted to make sure you guys had security on call."

"Lucky us," I can't help but scowl. I don't believe Sylian wants to make sure we're safe. He only wants to track our movements. To make sure we finish Logan so his "friends" at the NSA will continue to look the other way when it comes to his business dealings. Sylian is only interested in protecting his business and himself. There are no favors in Sylian's world.

"I'll be next door," Smith says, nodding at Mike before disappearing through a door at the edge of the room. It annoys me that Smith talks to Mike like he's in charge when he's not.

"Next door?" I ask.

"The place is a compound," Mike shrugs. "Different suites all connected to a central living area. Guess they do a lot of business in LA."

As soon as the door shuts, Mike's eyes shift to the ceiling. I follow his gaze. In the corner of the room, there's a camera. My eyes snap back to Mike, understanding.

We're being watched.

"Sometimes we just have to go with the flow, right?" Mike says. I understand what he means. They're watching us, and we have to wait until the opportune moment to make a break.

"Sometimes, we do," I tell him.

"This will all be over soon anyway," he adds.

"Yes," I answer. "It will."

LATER, Mike plugs his iPhone into a portable speaker, positioning it on the bathroom countertop. The bathroom is attached to the master suite we're staying in. The plush linens and fully-stocked soap dish make the bathroom look like a hotel. Not a small cog in a machine of criminal enterprise.

Mike puts my favorite playlist on blast. The volume is so loud my ears hurt. The first song up is Nick Drake, Pink Moon. One I've listened to a hundred times, but never this loud.

Mike pulls me into the shower with him and closes the door behind us.

"This is the only place I haven't found a camera," he says.

Hot water runs over my face, making me feel new.

"Guess even Sylian has boundaries," I tell him. "Why didn't you tell me we were being watched in the van?"

"They bugged my phone," Mike says, shaking his head. "I know they did. These guys have ears everywhere. Sylian was watching you in Europe. He knew where you were. Had somebody tailing you every step of the way. Smith told me as much."

"You and Smith are bros now."

"That's what *he* thinks," Mike snorts. "I swear the guy doesn't have a pal in this world. He's been talking non-stop about how he got into the business. How his older brother just got divorced. At this point I know his favorite sports team, top five fast food choices, and zodiac sign. But I got him to tell me about you, which is all I care about. I was going to shake him and disappear, but once he said Sylian was watching you I couldn't. In case they tried something, I had to be around to know where to find you."

"Sylian wants Logan dead as much as we do," I answer. "He's only tailing me to make sure the job is done."

Mike sighs. Leans against the tile wall. Runs a hand through his wet hair. It's a motion I've seen him make a thousand times since we've been together. One he does when he's thinking.

"Who says the job has to be done?"

My stomach turns. I don't like where this is going. "If we don't do it—"

"This is more complicated that when we started," Mike says. "Sylian... this... *enterprise*... they know too much about us. They're more dangerous than Logan."

"They'll leave us alone once he's gone," I say, not completely believing it myself.

"Will they?" Mike says. "Zoe, you don't have to do this.

We have a once in a lifetime opportunity to disappear. But we have to do it *now*."

"You can't be serious." The water is warm, but a cold shiver runs through my limbs. "We've come so far—"

"And now it's time to let Sylian finish the job. Your Mom is already abroad, hidden where they can't touch her. I know Smith's routine. I've already got a plan to get us out of here. Cassandra has promised me she can get us a plane to the island."

"You talked to *Cassandra?*" Now I *know* Mike is serious. He avoids interacting with Cassandra at all costs.

"I need to get you out of here," he says, taking my hands in his. "If we don't leave now, we might never be able to. They know where we work. Our social security numbers. They'll always be able to find us, unless we leave now."

"I can't."

"You won't."

"That too," I nod.

Mike puts his arms around me, holding me close. "Then let *me* go to Logan tomorrow," he whispers in my ear. "Not you. Let me do it."

This is what he's wanted the entire time. To make agree to let him go in my place.

"You'll be there," I say, reassuring. "I need you behind the scenes. I'm counting on you."

"You can run the trapdoor yourself," Mike says. "Put me on the inside and let me get it done."

"No," I say, simply.

"You don't understand what can happen," Mike says, fighting to keep his voice low. "What you're getting into—"

"I do know," I answer. "Of course I know. It's happening to *me*. You don't understand how it feels to be stalked like prey. I need to end this. And I know what it's going to take."

"But you don't!" He exclaims. "You don't know what it is because you've never lost anybody. Not really."

I lean my head against his chest, suddenly realizing I'm not the only one who feels misunderstood. Mike parents died tragically when he was young. He's had a hard life. Seen terrible things I'll never understand.

"I'm sorry," I tell him, softening. "But I have to do this."

"You fucking frustrate me," he sighs, releasing me.

"Yeah," I laugh. "Better get used to it. You made the horrible mistake of marrying me, so if I don't die tomorrow, you're going to be frustrated for a long time."

Mike looks at me like I've slapped him. "Marrying you wasn't a mistake." His eyes scan my face like he's memorizing it. "That was the best decision of my life."

He pulls me toward him and kisses me so hard I can't think of anything but his lips against mine. I wrap my arms around him, fading into the moment like it's my last, just in case I fail tomorrow. Just in case I fail, and never get the chance to fade into him again.

23

LOGAN

U*nited Airlines Flight 181, over the Atlantic Ocean.*

THANKS FOR THIS, *Zoe*, I think. A stewardess is engaging in annoying chit-chat with the passenger in front of me. This is my first time flying commercial in years. My seat is in first class, but the difference between flying private and commercial is a stark one. A fake passport helped me find my way onto the plane. I seriously debated chartering a jet, but the toll on my personal savings would be extreme. Funny, how spending money hits you differently when the funds are your own and not someone else's.

The passenger in front of me shifts, and I realize he's holding hands with the woman next to him. From their conversation with the stewardess, it's clear they've just gotten married. They're coming back from a honeymoon.

I look away.

The plastic blind squeaks as I open the cover on the window, fixating on the night sky. A few rays of sunlight peak out beyond the horizon. We've crossed three time zones already.

As much as I try to ignore them, I can't stop glancing back at the couple in front of me. I wonder what it feels like to trust yourself with another person. I've never seen what benefit might be worth such a risk. Whatever the feeling is, it must be a big one.

The truth is, I've never been close to anyone. Not really. That's what's so strange about the game Zoe's created for me. Even though it's a dangerous one, it makes me feel seen in some way. The trouble she had to go to in order to explore my history was no small task. The thought strikes me before I can push it away:

The person who is most interested in me in this world is the one who wants to destroy me.

I don't blame her of course. I'm shocked it took her this long. I make it a practice to obliterate my enemies long before they have the chance to turn on me. As much as I hate to admit it, Zoe is a worthy adversary. She might beat me tomorrow.

And if she does, I'll lose the only person in this world I care about:

Me.

I don't know what it would be like, to die. I've never come close. I'm always two steps ahead. It's an exhausting way to live. Maybe I'll be at peace, if Zoe wins. If she loses, I'll have to find another subject. Some other version of her represented by another woman, with whom I'll make the same mistakes. The cycle will repeat, again and again, because I don't know any other way to exist.

You will beat Zoe, I tell myself. *She will lose, like they always do. And you will win, like you always do.*

I close my eyes, and see Mia's face, swimming in the dark

place I go to when I sleep. It's impossible not to wonder where she is, and what she's doing. Not because I care, but because I want to know what ripple effect my choices have caused. When I defeat my enemies, am I really winning? Or does it only appear that way in the moment? Maybe, in some world beyond this one, Mia is living as an idea— a new version of her old self.

Yes, I killed her that day I left her on the island. But I also killed the old version of me. The child I once was. I killed him slowly, dying by a thousand cuts. It started the moment I took off in that sailboat, leaving Mia behind on a rock in the middle of the sea.

She'll find a way off the island, I lied to myself that day. *She's a genius, after all. I'm allowed to take the boat. It's mine.*

It was the first lie I ever told myself, and it was followed by a hundred bigger lies, day after day, in the weeks— the months— the *years*— that followed. I replaced myself like a jigsaw puzzle. One piece at a time, I destroyed the parts of myself that made me vulnerable, until the picture on the puzzle was something new. Something safer. It's an image I can't deviate from. The image is me, now.

I imagine Mia starting over in some new, celestial plane, and suddenly I'm jealous of her. I picture her as a being made of light, skipping comets over milky ways like rocks on a pond. In my dream, she is free and happy, able to grow and change. She turns into a plant, her arms like vines, reaching away from me at some person I can't see. She's not static, but evergreen. Always blooming, new flowers blossoming from her branches. She sheds her petals at night, and when the sun rises, new ones bloom in their place.

This version of Mia is expansive, so much more than who she used to be. The new Mia is fresh and adaptable, free from mistakes, rooted forever in the purity of the soil she tended to in the life she once had. In the place where she lives, now, she has the chance to be new again. A chance to start over.

A chance I wish I could have, but will never get.

WHEN I WAKE UP, we're flying over land. All dreams of Mia are washed away in the newness of the morning. The United States, promiser of freedom, sprawls beneath the plane window in a mess of jagged waterways and city lights. It won't be long until we touch down at LAX. This will be the final game between Zoe and me. Her letter promised me as much.

My legs stretch as I stand, reaching for the overhead bin. My backpack feels heavier than it did hours ago. Jet lag. I'm weak. I need to rest before my next test. I sit down, unzipping the pack and pulling out Zoe's most recent clue. The one I retrieved from the floor tile in the place where Mia died.

The envelope is warped in some places from exposure to the salt air, and the top is uneven from where I ripped it open. But the poem inside is unharmed, still perfectly legible. A glance behind me tells me the passengers over my shoulder— and elderly man and middle-aged woman— are sleeping. They won't be a bother. After making sure no one is watching, I unfold the poem and begin to read. I've read it a dozen times in the last twenty-four hours. But one more look won't hurt. It's my last connection to Zoe. The final, single thread that ties us together.

"You want your case,
    Of course you do,
    Trust in this,
    Your final clue.

Your case is in
    a place we met,
    Not the park,
    Lest you forget.

This is where
    You saw me first,
    Uninvited—
    A guest that hurt.

Check in on time,
    Avoid the fumes,
    Come at night,
    Clair de Lune.

The room that's yours
    Will be on hold
    You'll find it if
    You do as told.

Answer questions,
    Left or right,
    Get them wrong,
    We'll use our might.

To ruin what
    you love the most
    One at a time—

Your case is toast.

Hope you knew,
> *The ones you harmed,*
> *Otherwise—*
> *Please be alarmed.*

THE FIRST HALF of the clue provides easy directions to the next location. It's simple to decipher using my shared history with Zoe.

Your case is in
> *a place we met,*
> *Not the park,*
> *Lest you forget.*

This is where
> *You saw me first,*
> *Uninvited—*
> *A guest that hurt.*

Zoe and I met in person at Yosemite, but had encountered each other once prior. After our conversations online, I stopped by the hotel she worked at in Santa Monica. She didn't *know* it was me, of course. But I made sure to make my impression. I'm surprised she would want our final to occur at a place she holds so dear. As the manager of the hotel, Zoe treats it like her own home. It's beloved—sacred—to her.

I've scheduled my flight to arrive before sunset, because the poem is explicit about the timing:

Check in on time,
   Avoid the fumes,
   Come at night,
   Clair de Lune.

"Clair de Lune" references not just the moon and the arrival time, but the hotel's name itself: the Hotel Delune.

There's a buzzing sound overhead, and the fasten seat-belts sign turns on. My buckle clicks into place as I lean back, thinking about Zoe's letter. When I met Zoe, my goal was to turn her into someone who sees the world the way I do. She had so much promise. So much potential. Together, we could have lived as a pair, brought together by mutual self-interest.

In front of me, the married couple shifts in their seats. The woman leans her head on the man's shoulder.

Zoe and I could have had something. We would never have been like that married couple, of course. Whatever that feeling is, it's not what I'm interested in it. But we *could* have shared a connection unique and all our own. Something that didn't expect much of either one of us. No sacrifice. No altruism. Just two species meeting, seeing benefit for both and living together until the arrangement no longer makes sense.

But Zoe didn't see the possibility. Didn't live up to her promise. Yes, I'm looking forward to seeing her. To finishing this, once and for all.

24

ZOE

S anta Monica.

THE HOTEL DELUNE is one of my favorite places in the world. And it's falling apart.

I'm standing in front of it, holding Mike's hand. A chain link fence surrounds the perimeter, a sign on the metal reading "*Under New Ownership*." The wooden window-frames are splintered, the glass panes they used to hold replaced by sheets of particle board. Shingles hang from the roof in a desperate attempt to stay in place. If buildings could cry, we'd be drenched.

"Told you," Mike says. We're standing under a shadow cast by a rotting wooden awning. The sun is already setting, and a golden glow behind the hotel's facade adds an ominous overtone to the moment. "It's worse than when you left."

"That's alright," I say, unbothered. "It's mine now. Once this is over, anything is possible. This is its final sacrifice."

"We could've picked a tear-down," Mike answers. "Something we didn't care about."

I shake my head. "No, it had to be here."

I haven't told Mike, but when I learned that Logan masqueraded as a guest to meet me at the hotel without my knowledge, I felt violated. He'd intruded on a space I loved, and tried to make it his own. Now, I'm ready to remake it. When he's gone from this world, no longer able to insert himself into my life, I'll know it's time to start rebuilding the hotel. Thanks to Cassandra, we have the money to start fresh. She purchased the hotel for us at a bargain price. As the hotel's manager, I was constantly frustrated by the owner's unwillingness to make necessary repairs. It was as if I watching the place slowly die, and the owner refused to give it medical attention. Now, Mike and I are the owners.

This hotel represents my second chance. My new life. I've owned it for a year, but never touched a renovation. From the moment Cassandra purchased it for us, I've let it sit. Let it rot. Closed it to guests, waiting, because there's only one guest I'm interested in entertaining.

I want him to check in, and never check out.

"How long do we have?" Mike asks.

"Until sundown."

"You're sure I can't talk you into making a break for it? You could leave me here, Zoe. I'd get it done."

I know he would. But it has to be me.

"Show me the maze," I tell him.

Mike sighs, leading me to the front door. It opens with a creaking, painful sound. The scent of sawdust hangs in the air, hinting at something new built within.

I'm eager to see what he's built. Eager to get into position.

To end my old life, and start again— new.

25

LOGAN

S*anta Monica.*

THE HOTEL DELUNE is worse for wear. When I arrive, it takes extracting a pair of wire-cutters from my backpack to get through the chain-link fence surrounding the hotel's perimeter. I've made sure to pack every useful item at my disposal. Who knows what surprises Zoe has planned.

The monolithic building stares down at me as I approach the front entrance, its exterior lanterns arranged in a line. The pattern they trace curves upward, making it look as if the hotel is smiling at my approach. The jagged teeth call me onward. Double doors at the front entrance spiral upward, their wooden facades embodying the same decaying grandeur as the rest of the structure. They're unlocked. A simple push opens them with ease.

A few steps bring me into the hotel lobby— the belly of the beast. It's exactly as I remember it, but faded somehow.

It's as if the entire place has been laid beneath a sepia filter, turning what used to be vibrant into watered-down shades of taupe and grey.

The furniture in the sitting room is arranged in a common layout— two lush couches flanking an ornate coffee table. The couches have been covered in plastic, but the table sits alone, its face exposed to the elements. I run my finger over it. Nothing but dust. Overhead, cobwebs hang from the ceiling, a tangled mess.

Gee, Zoe. You've really let the place go.

The poem requested I check in, so I proceed to the most logical point of contact: the guest services counter. A massive, ornate desk serves as its centerpiece. Hand-carved flowers curve up the desk's front, and for a moment I think of how Mia appeared in my dream, her arms turned to blossoms. I push the thought away.

Leaning over the desk, I don't notice anything unusual. Discarded papers. A few folders. Stains from coffee cups, making circles on the glass top. Then, I spot a large, bronze key.

It's old— probably original to the building. The quality of the metal is patchy, dull in some places and shiny in others. There's a strip of paper tied to its handle, secured with a piece of red string. A single phrase is scrawled on its surface:

Find the room. I'm there.

This key is meant for me. The familiar handwriting tells me so. I grab it and head to the stairs, ready to try each room to see where it belongs. But when I reach the second floor landing, everything has changed.

The hallway is dark, and there's no doors, here. The rooms have been sealed off, their doors covered in dry wall, creating a single, solid wall. It runs the length of the corridor, an arrow painted on its surface, pointing me toward a dead end.

The change makes me pause. What awaits me? I pull out the poem, reading the latter half again with precision:

> *The room that's yours*
> > *Will be on hold*
> > *You'll find it if*
> > *You do as told.*
> > *Answer questions,*
> > *Left or right,*
> > *Get them wrong,*
> > *We'll use our might.*
> > *To ruin what*
> > *you love the most*
> > *One at a time—*
> > *Your case is toast.*
> > *Hope you knew,*
> > *The ones you harmed,*
> > *Otherwise—*
> > *Please be alarmed.*

Within this context, the poem takes on new meeting. The Delune is not a hotel anymore.

It's a maze, I think. They've allowed certain rooms to stay intact, and if I can only find the correct one, I'll also find Zoe.

I follow the red arrow to the end of the hall, where I hit a dead end. My fingers trace the wallpaper on either side, looking for a way forward where there isn't one. Then, a crackling noise from in front of me. A picture frame I'd overlooked come to life. What I'd though was a painting of a vase of flowers becomes something else: A monitor.

On the screen is Zoe's face, staring back at me, presumably in real time.

"You made it," she says to me, voice even. She's sitting in a room with a lush, four-poster bed behind her. The wood-paneling tells me it's a room here in the hotel. In the corner, there's a fireplace, flames crackling within, making shadows dance over her shoulder.

"How do I know this wasn't pre-recorded?" I ask her.

"What proof do you need?"

"Write down your name and show it to me."

She pauses. Walks to a desk next to the bed. Grabs a sheet of paper and a pen. She writes something down on it, then leans over to the camera, letting the paper flood the screen. The words on the page aren't her name.

"'Fuck off, Logan," I read aloud.

"Proof enough?" She asks.

"It'll do," I smile. "You picked the hotel. I'd like to think it's because you always secretly wanted to be here with me." I lean into the frame, looking for the camera embedded within. She can see me. I know she can. "What's your plan, Zoe?"

She speaks, the words like chalk, dry and rehearsed. "With each hall, you'll answer yes or no. If you get the question right, you'll be led—"

"That's not what I mean," I cut her off. "The plan. You're going to try to kill me?"

"You'll be led to the room—"

"Don't you understand that's why I chose you?" She stops speaking, waiting. Watching. "You could set yourself free, Zoe. You have so much potential. To be like me. To be *with* me. Together, we could have been great."

"If you get the answer wrong," she continues, ignoring me. "You lose an item."

This gives me pause. "An item?"

She nods, reaching under the bed and pulling out a familiar object. It's my suitcase. The place where I keep my souvenirs. My collection.

"The bank was a lie?" I ask, acid churning in my throat.

"I like to think of it more like theatre," she smiles. "We knew you'd look. Just wanted you to look in the wrong place."

"You are playing with fire," I tell her, the words soft and sad.

"No," Zoe says. "You are." She opens the suitcase and pulls out an item from my collection. It's a compass. One I stole from a forest ranger I killed not so long ago.

"This belonged to Brock?" Zoe asks. I don't answer. She already knows it was his or she wouldn't have chosen it. She nods as if I've agreed with her and then, in one terrible, fleeting moment, tosses the compass into the fireplace. The flames grow taller, delighting in the meal they've just consumed. The compass disappears into the smoldering tomb, irretrievable and forever forgotten.

I bite my tongue to stop from screaming. My Mother's affinity for collectibles manifests differently for me, but it's there all the same. Each of these items is irreplaceable. Each represents a time I was unstoppable. They are tangible proof of my power to overcome. My ability to change my environment and destroy my enemies. Without these items, it's as if those moments never happened. No record of my triumphs exists without them.

"When I get to that room," I tell her, "I'll throw *you* into the fireplace, and watch you burn."

"Come and get me," she says. The screen goes black.

All is still and silent for a moment, but then music echoes from speakers in the corner of the room. It's the jeopardy theme song, but it's been distorted. It plays in a twisted, minor key. White letters appear on the monitor. They read, simply:

"How many children did Brock have? Left for one. Right for two."

It takes me a second to place the name. I'm still thinking about my suitcase, alone with Zoe, the contents within at risk. But then, I turn my focus to what's in front of me. *Brock.* The forest ranger. An easy kill. He let his guard down so willingly.

Did Brock *have* children? He must have mentioned it on the tour. How would I know? Why would I care? Does anyone bother to listen to the mundane details about others, when they're too busy living a life of their own?

Zoe seems determined to use this experience to make a point. Some blathering, meaningless lesson about how I'm to live. Whatever it is, it's lost on me. I take a chance and turn left.

There's nothing but a wall in front of me. Still, my hand runs over the paper, looking for anything. Then, I notice a statue in the corner. It's a modern, machine-produced copy of an original, portraying an explorer holding a compass. I reach for the compass. The explorer's hand shifts with ease, and I realize it's a lever.

I pull it and the wall opens, revealing another hallway. It looks the same as the previous hallway, with one major difference: there's a door at the end. I run toward it, take a breath, and turn the handle.

It opens. The room within has all the same trappings as the one Zoe was in, but she's not there. Instead, another monitor is mounted on the wall, displaying the same, chunky white letters. They disappear with a crackle, revealing Zoe. She smiles at me from the screen.

"Wrong answer," she says, rifling through my suitcase. She pulls out a man's belt. We both know who it belongs to.

"Rick," she says, her eyes watering at the mention of the name of Mike's best man. I didn't kill him— not directly, anyway. But I set the scene. Made sure the necessary elements were in place. I spent weeks before the main event pressuring him financially by masquerading as debt collectors. Sending him hate mail, pretending to be someone who knew about his secret love life, threatening to tell everyone he knew. I pushed him to the brink. Once their party was off the island, I went back and retrieved an item of Rick's to remind me of what I'd done. When I noticed his belt poking out of the sand, it seemed only right to claim it as my own.

"Did you kill him?" She asks, her voice urgent.

"Why should I tell you?" I enjoy that she'll never know the truth.

She pauses, then tosses the wallet into the fire. I resist the urge to break the screen. It goes black, and new words appear.

"*What artist performed Rick's favorite song? Left for David Bowie. Right for Train.*"

The question is a joke. It's as if Zoe thinks she can make these people *real* to me. But what she doesn't understand is that no one is real to me. People, in my eyes, are tools. A means to an end.

I guess left again, turning down the hall and stopping at another door. There's a monitor on its surface, embedded into the wood. The static gives way to a black background. Letters appear.

"*Correct. The door you want is purple.*"

The door opens with a popping sound, with no

assistance from me. Suddenly, it occurs to me that Zoe isn't alone in this hotel. Someone must be running the electrical system and rigging the game. And there's no one Zoe would trust to do it, except for Mike.

He's here. And if I can get to him... I can get to her.

T *he Top Floor.*

EVEN ACROSS A MONITOR, I can tell: Logan's face turns to ash when I drop the compass in the fire. He loves these objects as much as he can love anything. They mean the world to him. He will put his own life in danger, to collect these valuables.

And that's what's going to lead him right to me.

I glance up at a camera in the corner. Mike is watching me from the other side. I can hear his voice in my ear— can sense him telling me to stick to the plan.

We're so close to freedom. So close to winning.

I check the monitor again and watch as Logan proceeds down the hall, following the directions from the screen. In another location, Mike operates the maze, activating different sections when the time is right.

Logan is playing by our rules, I think. *It feels too easy.*

Just then, Logan turns around. He reaches in his bag,

removing something. I step closer to the screen, and can just make out the outline of a gun. Four loud bangs echo across the hallway, and in a flurry of static, my cameras go dark.

Logan's gone off script. He doesn't want us to know his next move. Which can only mean one thing: it's a dangerous one.

27

LOGAN

T*he Hallway.*

I MAKE my way down the corridor, blasting every camera in my path. The path requires me to reload twice. They've rigged the place with cameras in every corner. I don't want them to know where I'm going, so I make a turn in the opposite direction, take out a flurry of cameras, then double-back the way I came. By the time they reach the area, I'll be gone.

It takes some knocking on the drywall, but eventually, a hollow sound rings back at me. There's a space behind the wall. These walls were newly built, a temporary installation meant to keep me on course. The entire interior of the hotel is a false set. Like the paper-thin walls in a haunted house pop-up good for one weekend only, these walls are a lie.

My fist bleeds as I punch my way through the drywall, but I don't care. This is my best chance of evading Mike and Zoe's surveillance. Punch after punch, my knuckles cry out. Finally, a hole opens. I tear it apart, enlarging the space so it's big enough to fit most of my body. Then, I worm my way inside, sneaking into the corridor behind. I'm in the original hotel now. The walls are wood paneling, not crumbling dry wall. I make my way down the hall, moving swiftly, sticking to the original layout of the hotel and avoiding those areas that have been altered.

Finally, I find an unlocked room. I sneak inside, pulling out my laptop and logging onto my hotspot. I need to figure out where the electrical signals are coming from. Mike's running this game from somewhere, and because the cameras are operating remotely, he'll leave a fingerprint behind.

It takes some searching, but I find it. There's a signal coming from downstairs, in the electrical room. Mike must be hiding there.

Perfect, I think, happy for the opportunity. They couldn't have made it easier to kill two birds with one stone. My laptop slams shut as I hurry down the corridor. I've looked up the original plans for the building, and found that there's a service staircase at the end of each hall.

When I reach the end of the corridor, the service staircase is there, waiting for me as promised. I slip inside and pound down the levels four steps at a time, feeling the air change as I descend to a level lower than the lobby. This is the maintenance area, limited to the underground portion of the hotel.

I open a door marked "*Employees Only,*" passing the servant's kitchen and the custodial closet. Then, at the end of the hall, I spot it.

The electrical room.

My breath catches in my throat. This is where Mike is running the game. Where he sits, waiting, like prey.

My eyes scan the corridor. There's no cameras, here.

They haven't thought to protect this area. They probably never considered I would evade their meager surveillance attempts, or that if I did, I'd look for Mike. Mike was likely more concerned with ensuring Zoe's safety than his own.

Tsk, tsk, I think. *This is why I avoid such entanglements.*

I slip my shoes off, leaving them further down the hall. I don't want Mike to hear my footsteps and sense my approach. When I reach the door to the electrical room, I pause, pressing my ear against it.

Mike's voice echoes from inside. He's on the phone.

".... Don't know," he says, the heavy timber of his words reaching out across the hall. The words are broken and I can't make out complete sentences, but I know it's him. From the snippets of conversation I can hear, it's obvious Zoe is warning him I've taken out the security cameras.

"Wasn't a good idea—" he mutters. How right he is about that. "— Should've planned it differently." He pauses. Then, his voice rises, louder. They're fighting. "I *told* you we should've gotten out while we still could!"

Now that I've confirmed the voice belongs to Mike, I waste no more time. A quick search of my bag provides what I'm looking for. The grenade is older, not a recent model. It's from a private stash I keep in Germany, built over many years of working for Sylian. Sylian didn't mind when older weapons went missing— a hazard of doing business with thieves. Before exiting Europe, I thought it might be wise to stop at my stockpile and remove some select resources. Turns out, I was right.

With care, I test the doorknob to the electrical room. It turns in my hand. They've left it unlocked. Using my teeth, I pull the pin out of the grenade and toss it behind me, running down the hall as fast as I can. I'm halfway to the stairs when the boom of an explosion ripples through the air, leaving my ears ringing. By the time I duck for cover, the job is done.

Shattered glass floods the corridor. Warped metal shapes make themselves known behind heavy dust. A glance down the hallway shows nothing but rubble where the room used to be. Somewhere under those stones and bricks, Mike's corpse lies in a pile, defeated before he even knew what was happening. They'll dig him out later, no doubt, but Zoe will be dead by then too. She'll never see them excavate him. Never see what her actions have caused. It's enough to make me want to let her live a little longer, but it's too risky a choice. Zoe dies tonight.

The lights are out, and the hallway is coated in darkness. Another happy side effect of destroying the electrical room. With a single decision, I've turned the tables in my favor. Their game won't work without an electrical system allowing them to open and close doors. The maze is no longer operable.

Mike is dead.

Zoe is sitting alone, defenseless, in a room with a purple door.

And I'm about to win the game.

28

ZOE

The Room With A Purple Door.

I'M TALKING to Mike on the hotel phone that's hard-wired into the wall when the line goes dead. The buttons on the phone lose their color. Sconces on the wall plummet into darkness.

The power is out.

Logan must have cut us off from the main line. I can't see him. Can't hear him. But I know what his next move will be.

He'll skip the rest of the maze. All he has to do is search the rooms until he finds one with a purple door.

He's coming for me.

T*he Upper Floor.*

I'VE BUSTED through the remainder of the maze. Without the electrical system in play, the doors are easy to open. There's no live wires operating the mechanical hinges that kept them shut. No black screen deciding my direction. Walking through the false walls makes the maze seem even more ridiculous. It's like watching a clown take off his costume. Disturbing, and a little sad.

Another door cracks as I break it down. Behind the door sits another vacant hotel room, a screen hanging from the ceiling. It's a dead end. This is the wrong direction. I turn back the way I came. The hallway ends in false wall. I push it open with ease, revealing another a corridor.

A corridor with five doors. All painted different colors.

Hello, Zoe, I think.

There's a yellow door on my left. A red door on my right.

A blue door down the hall. But I'm only interested in one: a purple door, in the middle of the hall.

My gun is already drawn, resting in my hand with ease as I approach the door. The gold key I found at the front desk slides into the lock— it's a perfect fit. Tumblers turn. The door screams as I kick it open. I'm half-expecting some kind of trap. Instead, what's in the room is simple. A scene I've been waiting for.

Zoe sits on the bed, frozen. In front of her is my suitcase, wide open, precious objects from my past displayed like knick-knacks in a pawn shop. Zoe doesn't move. If I didn't know better, I'd think the visual was a painting, like the ones that hang on the hotel walls. A still life, forever immovable. But then, Zoe speaks.

"You made it."

She doesn't try to move. Doesn't attempt to run away. She barely flinches as I raise my gun in the air and point it right at her head, squeezing the trigger tight. There's a familiar burst from the end of my arm as the bullet releases itself, heading straight for my target, ready to hit its mark.

30

ZOE

T*he Bed.*

I DIDN'T EXPECT him to shoot me so soon.

I thought we'd talk, at least. Nobody loves a game like Logan. I figured he'd want to play with his meal. Enjoy time with his prey before eating it. Instead, he's cut right to the chase. It's an action that tells me I've pushed him to edge. He's desperate. Afraid. No longer one that can afford to enjoy the hunt.

I don't move. Don't flinch. I know where the bullet is going.

Because this is still my game.

There's a muffled, pattering sound as the bullet hits the barrier in front of me. Mike and I planned it this way. I'd debated taking the extra precaution, because I worried Logan would notice the clear, plastic shield. But Mike insisted. Now, I'm glad he did.

Logan steps forward, confusion etched in his eyes. He

reaches out and touches the false wall in front of him. It's all that stands between him and I, and it stretches the entire length and height of the room. It reminds me of one of those plastic dividers organized people put in drawers, keeping bras away from panties, and panties away from mittens. Logan and I are separated, unable to cross the divide.

"Bulletproof," he says under his breath, still touching the wall. "It's expensive."

"I have a very wealthy benefactor," I tell him, smiling. "I believe you've worked with her before?" He doesn't answer, searching his mental records for wealthy contacts.

"Cassandra," I say, clarifying the point. Now that I have Logan in my clutches, it's safe to reveal her involvement. She'd *want* him to know. Later, she'll ask me to describe the look on his face when I told him. I try to record it to memory. It's a satisfying one.

"The girls teaming up," he smiles at me. "Adorable."

He starts to back out of the room, but I'm two steps ahead of him. Below my feet is a simple rope, attached to a more complicated pulley system that's wired through the attic. I pull it, and another bulletproof shield drops in behind him, cutting him off from the door through which he entered.

"It's a puzzle box," I say. "Fascinating things. Don't require electricity, which is nice. But then again it would be grand to have some lights on, don't you think?"

"Why don't you ask Mike?" Logan's face lights up. "His body is lying at the bottom of the electrical room, covered in rubble. He's dead. No matter what you do to me, you've already lost."

He waits for my reaction. "Alright," I tell him. "I *will* ask Mike." My fingers search the bedside table for my cell phone, the same burner I kept with me throughout Europe. I let it ring once before the line goes live. "Do it," I say.

There's a moment, then— the lights come on. The sound of multiple generators purring fills the room. Every device in the room leaps to life. There's a screen in the corner. I point to it, grabbing the remote off the bedside table. I click through the surveillance screens, stopping at the roof.

There's Mike, safe and sound, a bank of computers glowing in front of him. He's positioned on the roof, in front of the multiple backup generators we installed. When he sees the camera is live, he walks straight up to it and flips Logan the bird. Then he does it again. And again. He throws in a little dance, like the kind football stars do in the end-zone. He's really enjoying the moment, and I can't blame him one bit.

"I heard his voice," Logan says. "In the electrical room."

"Yes, that," I smile. "*That* was pre-recorded. Maybe you should have asked him to write your name on a piece of paper?"

Logan goes quiet. His eyes scan the cage he's in. Above, him, there's the same bulletproof barrier, sealing him inside. Beneath his shoes— carpet.

"The floor?" He asks, already knowing the answer.

"You can try," I encourage. He bends down and rips up the carpet. There's more of the same plexiglass, sealing him in tight. He nods. He knew it would be there.

"What's the plan now, Zoe?" He says, looking deep into my eyes. "You don't have it in you to kill me."

"Actually, I do," I tell him. "And that's what scares me. I'd like to kill you myself. To end this with my own two hands. But I'm afraid I won't be the same afterward. I don't want to become *like* you. Don't want to end up where you wished I

would. It's a bit of a puzzle, actually. One I've been considering for awhile."

"The ultimate game," Logan nods.

"It's one you've played before," I tell him. "One I think
you lost."

"What's your move?" He says. For a moment, his face is
childlike. As if there's some genuine piece of him that wants
to know how to escape. A small, sliver of his soul that wants
redemption. It grabs at me, but I know I can't trust it.

"It's not my move," I tell him. "It's *your* move."

"Mine?"

"Look in the corner."

He does. There's a computer, there. His eyes widen at the
sight. I've given him his best weapon. He bends down to
examine it, hitting return on the keyboard. The screen
lights up.

"You'll find it's unbreakable," I tell him. "You won't be
able to access any other programs except the one we've
opened for you. No going to the dark web. No calling in a
favor. A very capable friend of mine rigged it." I pause for
effect. "I helped Gabrielle get a new job, recently, so I guess
you could say she owed me."

Logan stares at the screen. He reads what's present,
there.

"And if I don't send it?" He asks.

I stand, walking toward the bulletproof shield. "The
funny thing about setting off grenades in hotels is that you
cant really control what you hit. You may not know this, but
you struck the main gas line."

"What a coincidence," Logan snarls.

"The insurance company is going to think so," I tell him.
"You gave us the idea, actually, with what you did to Lucija

and Andre's house. So, I guess we owe you a thank you for that."

Logan frown, disgusted.

"You have about five minutes before the gas pressure builds and connects with the pilot light," I continue. As I speak, a timer lights up on a screen at the end of Logan's cage.

"Send the document before that timer goes off, and we won't light the pilot. You'll live to see another day... With the appropriate consequences, of course. Decline, and you can burn with the building, undone by the very people you tried to destroy. Not just me, but Mike. And Cassandra. And Gabrielle. And Mia. And Rick. And Brock. And everyone represented here."

I grab the suitcase with Logan's trinkets and flip it over, letting them fall across the floor. He flinches at the sight of his precious souvenirs being so mishandled.

"You're going to destroy the hotel you love?" He asks.

"I'm going to start over," I tell him. "I'm going to start new, without you."

He pauses, then walks over to the glass. If it weren't for the divider, we'd be nose to nose.

"You know this is as good as killing me yourself," he says. "I can't do it."

"No," I tell him, looking into cold, never-ending sea within his irises. "Don't pretend you can't. Somewhere in there, there's a version of you who can. Find him. Or don't. The choice is yours."

With that, I turn my back on Logan— on Johann— on all the other presentations of self he's offered. My steps are noiseless on the plush carpet as I walk toward the window, pushing it open and pulling down the fire escape ladder.

I look back at Logan one more time before descending. There's one more thing I have to say.

"Do you even know why we made the door purple?" I ask.

"What?"

"The door," I tell him. "We made it purple because that was her favorite color. That was Mia's favorite color."

Logan stares back at me. He's standing behind that plexiglass, lost and alone, trapped in a room of his own making.

He holds the key. I've designed it that way. But I know he'll never let himself out.

31

LOGAN

T*he Trap.*

As soon as Zoe disappears from view, the bulletproof barrier seems to close in on me, getting smaller by the second. There's a clattering noise as I dump my backpack out on the floor, laying out every tool at my disposal in a line. I try to break through the glass with a hammer— try to pull at the seams of the construction— but there's no use. It doesn't bend.

My eyes land on another grenade, laying on the floor. I consider trying to blast my way through the barrier, but if it's truly impenetrable, the explosion might stay contained to this cage and kill me on the spot.

The timer counts down. Four minutes. Then three.

Nothing here will help me, I think. Nothing but that computer, and what's on the screen.

I leap to keyboard and spend another minute trying to hack it, but it's completely locked. There's no way to break through, no matter how many override commands I enter, no matter how many tricks I try. The timer is down to two minutes. I'm running out of time.

All that's left is the document on the screen. The one I know I can't send. I've scanned through it, and it's a lengthy evidentiary file outlining everything I've ever done. There's pages of evidence attached. Photographs. News articles. Witness statements. My old identities are there, along with documents connecting different versions of myself to one another. Johann. Logan. And a million other incarnations of "*me*," all present and accounted for.

But that's not what makes this document un-sendable. No, it's the letter at the top, the one that says things I promised myself I would never say. I breeze through it, reading as fast I can. Lines of prominence stand out as I scan, their mere presence making me panic.

"*I am responsible for the deaths of faultless victims—*"

Faultless? These are people that harmed me. That wronged *me*. That ignored my prominence, my advances, my desires. And Zoe wants me to claim they were blameless and undeserving? Never.

"*Attached are known accounts of those I've harmed. I am also committed to cooperating and revealing the identities of those unaccounted for—*"

Zoe wants me to provide the names of others I've killed. The naivety is truly striking. She assumes I bothered to *know* their names. The woman at the bar who declined my offer to buy her a drink. The man who took my parking spot and didn't notice as I waited outside the store, then followed him on his long drive home. I am always asserting my power. Always equalizing where I can. Of course I don't know their names. I don't need to.

"*I agree to cooperate with law enforcement and would like to take this opportunity to apologize, although I acknowledge no apology can cure—"*

Apologize? I haven't apologized in twenty years. And I'm not about to start now.

The minutes have gotten away from me. A glance at the timer tells me I'm down to thirty seconds. Thirty seconds. I've let my life come to this.

My logic tells me I should just send the letter. Hit the button. Allow the police to come. Maybe feign some remorse and buy my way out with whatever connections I can muster. But this document is so extensive, the evidence so clear, it's unlikely I'll succeed. Sending this means a life-time in prison, or perhaps worse. A lifetime in prison I could handle. At least I'd *be* alive. Sylian might present a problem though, as he'll have connections on the inside. If he's set on making my life miserable there, he'll be able to do it with ease.

Maybe the gas explosion is a hoax, I think. But my mind flips back to the fire sprinkler on the island, and the acid that fell from the ceiling. Zoe meant it then. She means it now. The acid rain wasn't meant to harm me. It was her way of giving me fair warning.

Sending the document is the right move. It gives me opportunities to maneuver. To try and find the best deal. To live to fight another day.

There's a box for a signature at the bottom. I use the mouse to sign it. Then, I hover the mouse over the button at the bottom of the screen. The one marked "send." All I have to do is click.

There's ten seconds left on the timer. This is it. This is what I must do.

I'm about to hit "send," but then— for some reason— I think of Mia.

Purple was her favorite color.

I think about the dream I had with her in it. The one where she was a plant, blooming again and again. Free, and able to remake herself a thousand times. I would like to remake myself. But I'm not sure I can do it, here. There's some part of this experience— of being human— that I've never fully understood. Maybe, if I were able to bloom like Mia, I could grow into someone who understands. Maybe, on some celestial other plane, I could be a new me.

My attention turns back to the screen, and the document in front of me. I can't apologize, but I can do this. I take my hand away from the mouse. The send button looks back at me, but I don't hit it.

Instead, I open my arms wide and close my eyes, conjuring images of Mia, wanting that eternal, flowering version of her to be the last thing I ever see. Not because I love her— I'm not sure what that feels like— but simply because I want to solve the mystery of it. I want to understand the piece I've been missing— the thing that exists between Zoe and Mike. The feeling between that couple on the plane. The odd, incorrigible faith that made Mia believe in me even when I'd left her behind.

I want to understand what's missing inside of me— to find the absent element that makes me feel like I'm half a person, surrounded by others who are whole.

32

ZOE

O*utside.*

MIKE and I are standing outside when the hotel goes up in flames. It starts with an explosion in the basement— the pilot light really *was* wired to a timer, although Logan's grenade didn't *actually* burst a gas line. We did that ourselves. We planned the entire thing, because we knew he'd go looking for Mike in an attempt to out-maneuver the maze. Logan doesn't like to play by the rules, so all it took from us was guessing which ones he'd try to break.

The building rocks. Glass shatters. The sound of the boom makes my ears burn. Flames lick the outdoor walls, and I'm a little surprised by how quickly the entire thing goes up in orange and yellow light. It's an old building, featuring oil-based paints that haven't been updated in years. That, combined with the wood construction means it's perfect tinder. I'm surprised we haven't had a fire sooner.

The fire engines arrive, but not soon enough. By the

time they get there, my beloved hotel is a pile of ash.

"It's alright," Mike says. "Now, we can rebuild."

The firefighters search the building for any remains, and the process takes a few days. I don't relax until we get the call. "Dental records," Mike says. "It was him. It was Logan. He's really gone, Zoe."

I don't feel any satisfaction. This was a game I was forced to play. One I never asked for.

Still, as the weeks pass by, I do start to feel a sort of freedom. A weightlessness I'd forgotten I could know.

We turn over the evidence we've collected to the C.I.A. Turns out, they'd been watching Logan for awhile. We blame the entire hotel incident on Logan. Mike claims Logan trapped me both of us in the bulletproof room, and we managed to escape. They believe it. Why wouldn't they? He's an international criminal. A girl like me could hardly have outsmarted him. "You're lucky," one agent says to me.

I don't feel lucky.

We take care of Sylian with a simple phone call. Once he independently confirms Logan is dead, he leaves us alone.

"Sylian will be back," Mike says, a worried edge to his voice. "I can tell."

"I don't know," I answer, disagreeing. "We're not useful to Sylian anymore. He'll forget about us."

Mike doesn't believe me, and I wonder if he's suffering from PTSD. I've noticed that he looks around corners a little more carefully. He covers his computer camera with a post-it note, in case someone is watching. This experience has taught him that there's *always* someone watching.

But over time, even Mike starts to relax. We rebuild the hotel. The insurance doesn't give us much, because the building itself didn't appraise out. Apparently grand old mansions that have been allowed to fall into disrepair aren't what makes a property worthwhile. "It's the land," the insurance adjuster says to us. "That's what's worth something. If you have a problem with that, give us a call."

"The land?" Mike laughs. "Guess we'll call them if there's a tenacious weed."

"They're useless," I agree.

We rebuild anyway. When we get into unexpected trouble with the plumbing, it takes a distribution from Mike's furniture business and a gift from the limitless pockets of Cassandra to bail us out. I promise her this is the last one. She doesn't care. "What's the point of having money," she says, "If you can't use it to help out the people you love?"

Love, I think. Love is the thing Logan never understood. It's love that allows Mike and I to forgive Cassandra, and what makes her lend to us without question. It's love that makes Mike and I stay together through all the difficulties we've faced, even in in our stubbornness, even in our flaws.

When we finish the hotel, it's a stark, beautiful thing. We've built the new version with the old one in mind, paying homage to the original structure. Large, expansive windows line the lobby. Gold foiling on the tables in the guest rooms. The walls are framed by crown moldings so thick and ornate you can help but stare. We've added modern features, too, to keep guests comfortable. Outlets with USB ports, and a cafe in the lobby. Wall-mounted televisions with streaming services already provided. It's a marriage between old and new.

When the hotel is finally finished, we hold a party to celebrate the grand opening. My Mom and Oliver fly back from the island, sporting new tans and a painful collection of tropical shirts. Hundreds of people come to the event, and Mike and I stand on the hotel balcony, looking out at the front lawn, watching them make new memories on the property we own. It occurs to me that each person here is a part of something bigger. A tiny piece of the great everything. Every person, every tree, every life, every animal— all of it combines to make some bigger picture. I don't what Logan's role was supposed to be in that great, shifting image. I don't think he knew, either. Deciding to let himself go back to the source might have been the only good thing Logan ever did.

One thing I'm sure of, now, is that there's no such thing as predators. No such thing as prey. We all affect each other equally in ways we can't understand, each one of us, essential. We might feel small, sometimes, but every one of us can define our own path. We have the tools to survive. To defend in the face of danger. It's like Sylian said. The tiniest bacteria can take down the biggest lion, if it knows its own strength. That's half the battle— just knowing what kind of animal you are. At the end of the day, I wasn't an animal who could take a choice away from Logan— and he was not an animal who could make a better one.

After everything I've been through, I know what I can live with. I know where my strengths lie, and where my weakness hide. I'm not worried about being like Logan, anymore, because I've seen the very worst of myself and emerged intact, a whole, full person, exactly the one I was meant to be. And I don't just know *who* I am. I know who I'm better *with*.

Mike puts his arm around me, letting me lean my head on his shoulder.

"Everything's going to be okay, now," he says.

For the first time in a long time— I believe him.

THE END.

ALSO BY THIS AUTHOR

∼

Also by Valerie Brandy

Book One:

Animals We Are

Book Two:

Animals We Are: The Wolf & The Bee

∼

Formats

The entire *Animals We Are* series

is available in ebook, paperback, and audiobook.

AUTHOR MAILING LIST

Love the *Animals We Are* series and want more?

Sign up to receive alerts about new releases from this author, including special offers and discounts available to subscribers only.

Be the first to know about new releases!

To join the list, visit the author on social media, or stop by her website at:

www.valeriebrandy.com

ACKNOWLEDGMENTS

∼

To everyone I thanked in book one. You have my continued appreciation, love, and dedication.

ABOUT THE AUTHOR

Valerie Brandy is a screenwriter, director, actress, and author based in Los Angeles. As a screenwriter, she's worked for various studios and networks, both in feature length films and in television development. As an actress, she recurred on FX's Emmy-Winning show *Justified*.

Her award-winning feature film "*Lola's Last Letter*," which she wrote, directed, and starred in, was distributed by Sony's 'The Orchard' after a successful festival run. Brandy was nominated for a Best Principal Actress Award by Los Angeles Film Review for her compelling performance in the film.

Her debut novel, "Animals We Are," was released in late 2019, and is the first in a thriller trilogy.

She graduated from UCLA in three years, with honors, as a prestigious Alumni Scholar.

To keep in touch or sign up for Valerie's mailing list, visit:

www.valeriebrandy.com